After several minutes, the exhausted Deane stared at the limp page of the notebook lying open on the camp table. Reading it over, it sounded as unbelievable on paper as it had in his mind.

"*For the record, I am not hallucinating. Tired, excited, a little confused, perhaps, but definitely NOT INSANE!*

Yet this morning, I saw an old Indian woman change into a jaguar! . . ."

AMAZING™ Books

AMAZING™ STORIES

JAGUAR!
by Morris Simon

TSR, Inc.™

Distributed to the book trade in the United States by Random House, Inc., and in Canada by Random House of Canada, Ltd.
Distributed in the United Kingdom by TSR UK, Ltd.

Distributed to the toy and hobby trade by regional distributors.

DUNGEONS & DRAGONS, ADVANCED DUNGEONS & DRAGONS, and AD&D are registered trademarks owned by TSR, Inc.

AMAZING, SUPER ENDLESS QUEST, PRODUCTS OF YOUR IMAGINATION, ONE-ON-ONE, and the TSR logo are trademarks owned by TSR, Inc.

First printing: September, 1985
Printed in the United States of America
Library of Congress Catalog Card Number: 85-51043
ISBN: 0-88038-256-2

9 8 7 6 5 4 3 2 1

TSR, Inc.
P.O. Box 756
Lake Geneva, WI 53147

TSR UK, Ltd.
The Mill, Rathmore Road
Cambridge CB1 4AD
United Kingdom

**TO WARD
FROM A BACK WARD
IN SPACE AND TIME**

PROLOGUE

The intercontinental airport at Merida, the largest city in Mexico's Yucatan Province, is always crowded in the early spring. The balmy days and cool nights provide relief from the steamy, suffocating heat of the Yucatan jungle for the *yanqui* visitors to the nearby ancient Mayan ruins.

Steven Deane let the stream of tourists from his economy flight out of Cozumel race ahead of him to the baggage dump. He knew it would take the jet-age stevedores a minimum of two hours to unload the rickety DC-7, whose bright Aztec designs hid its patched and battered aluminum skin.

To avoid the rush of excited tourists, Deane had handcarried his heavy leather B4 bag, which contained all of the personal gear he planned to need for the next twenty-four months. The large trunk with his research equipment could wait unclaimed until he had arranged for transportation to Monte Azul. The bulky bag weighed more than eighty pounds, but the young scientist hefted it as easily as if it were a briefcase. He had spent the last two months skindiving and beachcombing on the less crowded but more beautiful islands near Cozumel, and his athletic body was in its best condition since he played lacrosse in college.

He was already dressed for the field: comfortable but sturdy brogans, khaki work pants with large side-pockets, a fresh blue denim shirt, and a misshapen Panama hat with a faded madras band. His only requirement had been comfort; fashion had little or nothing to do with his taste in clothes.

Deane dodged into the airport lounge just inside the terminal and settled himself in a corner booth to wait for the crowd to thin. Enjoying the comparative quiet, he ordered a bottle of Dos Equii, which he paid for with his last American vacation money, a crumpled twenty-dollar bill from the bottom of a bulging side-pocket. He knew he would be watched for the first several months and wanted to give the Federales no real reason to deport him, as using black-market currency might. That way, he hoped he would be forgotten quickly by the authorities so that he could melt into the countryside near Monte Azul and do his work unhampered by officials who hated Americans but craved their dollars.

The linguist ignored the dingy glass with its promise of amoebic dysentery and drank the thick cold beer directly from the bottle. He leaned his head back on the cushioned booth and savored the beer and the respite from the airport's commotion. But a loud conversation disturbed his peace. It was coming from a table near one of the windows overlooking the main runway. A huge bear of a man, his back turned to Deane, was offering to sell some "original" Olmec sculptures to a middle-aged American couple seated across from him.

"These are the rarest and oldest of Mexican art treasures," the giant was explaining in a dramatic stage whisper. "Actual museum pieces which were, shall we say 'diverted,' from their intended destination!"

Deane chuckled. The man's English was thickly accented but nearly flawless, and he was using one of the most effective swindle techniques in the business: offering to sell stolen art treasures on the duty-free side of an airport. He had probably picked these two customers because of their clothes and jewelry, Deane noted, since tourists with expensive but flashy tastes are the preferred "marks" for the "shady bargain" routine.

"Olmec art is even more valuable than Mayan," the American woman whispered to her husband. Greed flashed across the man's well-scrubbed face as she added, "Archeologists think that the Olmecs were the original civilization in the entire Western Hemisphere. All those other cultures like Maya and Aztec would never have developed if they hadn't inherited all of the Olmecs' knowledge."

"What they say is true, Senora Gladden. Scientists who have studied the Olmec believe that they understood astronomy and irrigation long before the Maya. Their religion was just as complicated as those described by the Spanish conquistadores of the sixteenth century, although they lived more than three thousand years earlier!

"Where do you think the Olmec came from, Senor Faranza?" asked the blonde woman. She had the stringy, deliberately uncombed, frizzled hair first popularized by rock stars and soap goddesses, and later misappropriated by affluent freckled women in tennis skirts. This one appeared to be more intelligent than many.

"No one knows, Senora Gladden," the huge man replied. "A thousand years before the birth of Christ, they were already sculpting some of the finest pieces of art in Central America. There is no sign of gradual development, as you would find in other parts of the world. It is as if the Olmec appeared suddenly from nowhere, already knowing how to do things no one had ever attempted before."

"Isn't that one of the arguments behind those theories involving visits by ancient spacemen?" asked Mr. Gladden.

"Don't be silly, John. It's much more likely that visitors from Africa or Asia brought Olmec culture to Mexico," his wife interrupted.

"Good for you, lady," thought Deane, his interest in the conversation beginning to stir. "Now let's see if you can spot this guy's fake artifacts before your husband blows a bundle on a whim!"

"Excellent!" the dealer called Faranza exclaimed. "Your wife knows what she's talking about, Mr. Gladden. Let me show you an example of the influences which some artists and scientists believe came from China or Japan."

Something about the man's accent struck Deane. When the dealer reached under the table for a canvas valise, Deane caught a glimpse of his profile and recognized the classic beak-nosed Indian features immediately. Mayan! It was unusual for a true Yucatecan Mayan to be working as an airport hustler, even in Merida. Most of the confidence men were urban Mexicans or foreign nationals.

Faranza unzipped the valise and removed a small parcel wrapped in white tissue. He glanced suspiciously around as the two Americans shoved their drinks and appetizers aside. He then set the object in the center of the small cocktail table, handling it with dramatic caution that approached reverence. The dealer unwrapped the parcel with delicate and deliberate movements calculated to heighten the impact of his sales presentation.

Deane, thoroughly distracted and amused by the miniplay at the adjacent table, ordered another Dos Equii. The waitress appeared with the fresh bottle just as the object began to emerge from its white cocoon. Deane turned away from the dramatic moment to pay her. When he glanced back at the trio, his throat tightened. The wide-eyed couple from America was staring at one of the most beautiful pieces of original Olmec sculpture the scientist had ever seen!

It was a male figurine, carved from fine milky green jade in the unmistakable Olmec style. The long face with its Asiatic eyes was just as distinctive as the slender, three-dimensional "paper doll" appearance of the highly polished torso. Deane's own research on Olmec origins had acquainted him with the major collections throughout the world, and he knew most of the other existing Olmec artifacts from professional photographs. This particular statuette had not been copied from any he had ever seen, and it was much too fine to be an imitation.

The surprise of seeing such an exquisite museum piece on a plastic table in an airport lounge was more than Deane could suppress. Sliding from his booth, he approached the trio from behind the Mayan's broad back.

"Excuse me," he said in perfect Spanish, "but may I see that sculpture?"

The Mayan dealer whirled around to face Deane, a nervous look on his face. In a flash, he grabbed the figurine and the canvas bag, leaped up from his chair, upsetting it, and bounded out of the lounge. The two tourists stared dazedly at the abandoned pile of tissue paper on their table.

"Where did you meet that man?" Deane asked the couple in English. They looked up, startled at the sight of his sun-bleached golden hair and piercing blue eyes, as well as his unaccented American English.

The man scowled angrily, but his wife flashed a flirtatious smile at Deane as she studied his handsome features.

"Fake, huh? I thought so, but *John* would have bought it," she complained in scathing tones. "Are you American? Airport security?"

"Yes, from upstate New York," Deane answered, "but I'm not a policeman. I'm a linguist, and a specialist on Mayan and pre-Mayan languages, including whatever dialects the Olmec spoke. That's why I barged in on your conversation when I saw that sculpture."

"I didn't know linguists were also authorities in archeology," her husband said with thinly veiled hostility. Deane ignored the insulting tone.

"I'm just beginning a two-year survey of remote Mayan languages for the Mexican government. They want the survey to help develop education programs, but I'm more interested in pre-Mayan linguistic history, particularly Olmec," he explained. "For the past year, I've been studying every Olmec artifact I could find, and I know the style very well. That one he was trying to sell you was either a real one or one of the best imitations I've ever seen."

"Do you mean to tell me you scared that big guy away when he was about to sell me a genuine Olmec piece?" demanded Gladden. "And you thought he saved me money!" he snarled to his wife.

"Not money, just time," Deane corrected the irate man. "I'd say about twenty years in a Mexican jail for illegal smuggling of a national art treasure. Look over there, at the end of the bar."

The two followed Deane's nod. A small man in a stylish leather jacket and tan cotton slacks was speaking to the bartender. Leather Jacket glanced occasionally at the trio of Americans as he talked. There was no attempt to hide the fact that they were under surveillance.

"If I were you," Deane told his two companions, "I'd go to the gate and wait for your plane without talking to anyone except the ticket agent. Don't press your luck!"

He smiled at their dumbfounded expressions and went back to his table. By the time he had taken the first sip of his new beer, the frightened couple had slipped hastily out of the lounge and headed toward their gate. The undercover customs official gave Deane a curious look and rushed off behind them. The linguist waited a few minutes, then left a tip, and picked up his bag. Within ten minutes he was on the shuttle bus to the city.

Deane never stayed at the expensive tourist hotels in

Merida, preferring both the company and the prices at the ones patronized by Yucatecans. He was accustomed to the minor inconveniences that most American tourists pay high prices to avoid. The Yucatano was one of his favorite hotels. It was moderately priced by native standards, which meant very cheap to people like the Gladdens. The clientele was a mixture of traveling merchants, sightseeing peasants, and civil servants on holiday.

The clerk recognized him immediately. Not many Americans risked the native *barrio* sections of Merida to stay at the Yucatano. But then, no one who knew Deane considered him to be just another *yanqui*. He spoke Spanish better than most natives, although he could use their street slang if he chose to do so. Deane's command of the Indian dialects was even more impressive.

Deane had spent most of the past five years working and teaching for the Mexican government in both Tabasco and Campeche provinces, near the traditional Olmec heartland. He spoke at least a dozen obscure Mayan dialects as well as a few languages that were known only to isolated handfuls of speakers, such as Zoque and Mixtec, which were thought by some linguists, including Deane, to be close to the original tongue of the ancient Olmecs.

As a child of an American diplomat, Deane had grown up in Central America and was accustomed to everyone around him speaking several different languages. His natural linguistic ability led him to be recruited by the Central Intelligence Agency at seventeen, through his father's acquaintances in the Agency. But he quickly tired of the political intrigue and paramilitary games the CIA played in Latin America.

The Agency had offered to send him to college, but on their own terms. They were grooming him for a professional espionage career and wanted to dictate his selection of courses, even including his sports.

"I'm not a spy, and I'm not a mercenary, and I don't ever want to be either one of those things," he had told Jorges, his Agency link at the Langley, Virginia, headquarters. "I'm quitting the Company and going to school—for myself."

His flair for languages, sports, and computer science took him sailing through a bachelor's degree at Princeton and a doctoral program at Boston University. For his Ph.D. dissertation, he wrote a computer language translation program, which the State Department purchased with an unprecedented royalty contract even before it was accepted by the BU graduate school. In 1983, Deane started receiving more than four thousand dollars a month from his program. He promptly spent part of the first check on a one-way ticket to Mexico.

At first, the Mexican Government was suspicious of this bright young American with known CIA contacts throughout Central America. He never tried to soothe their paranoia, believing the less he said, the sooner they would leave him alone. The strategy worked; Deane was soon working wherever he liked in Maya or Olmec country, partly because the government was receiving some wonderful research at practically no cost, and partly because the Federal police saw no harm in keeping the one-time secret agent occupied within range of easy surveillance.

"There is a message for you, Mr. Deane," the nightclerk told him as he checked into the Yucatano at seven o'clock that evening.

"For me?" Deane was immediately curious. No one knew he was returning before April. The clerk handed him a folded note. Opening it, he read:

———

Please accept my gratitude for not reporting me to the authorities. If you will remain in your room this evening, I have something to discuss which will intrigue you.

Luis Faranza

Deane frowned. "Did you see the person who brought this message?" he asked the nightclerk.

"I'm sorry, but no, Senor. It was here when I came to work. Perhaps the dayclerk will remember. I can call her at home."

Deane hesitated, then shrugged. "No, don't do that. It's not that important." Taking the key, he climbed the creaking staircase. At Number 274, he turned the lock and entered the dark room, flicking on the lights as he shut the door.

"Welcome home, Senor Deane!"

The sudden voice startled him, although he recognized it immediately. The tall Mayan called Faranza was lying on the sagging bed, hands under his head and feet hanging off the other end.

"I'm early," Deane said in Spanish. "Who are you? Customs? Counterintelligence? Or just a crook?"

"Please, Mr. Deane!" Faranza interjected in English. "These walls are too thin for such demeaning insults. Perhaps you would find it, uh, easier to discuss our business in your native language."

"Talk, Faranza!" Deane demanded. "Whatever language you use, you have just five minutes, then you leave."

The giant Mayan sat up, swung his feet to the floor, and shrugged his shoulders.

"You may wish for it to take longer than that, Mr. Deane. I have learned many things about you since we met at the airport—many interesting things!"

"That's half a minute," Deane said coolly, his eyes watching the Mayan's every more. The young scientist remained standing, tensed, near the door.

"I shall come to the point immediately, Mr.—or do you prefer 'Dr.'?—Deane? It seems that we can help each other very greatly in the coming months."

"I'm waiting for the point, Faranza."

"Could you call me 'Luis?' Using one's family name is too cold. I will call you 'Steven.' " He pronounced it "Stay-ban," the Mexican short form of "Esteban."

"Three minutes, Faranza."

"As you wish." He sighed. "I want to show you where to find many more Olmec artifacts like the statuette you saw this afternoon. When you joined us so . . . abruptly . . . I thought at first you were a customs inspector. They hire Americans, you know. That's why I left the airport so rudely."

Deane's interest rose sharply, but he did not want Faranza to know it. "I have very little time for this kind of business, Faranza. I'm leaving tomorrow."

"For Monte Azul. I know of your research, Dr. Steven Deane," said the Mayan, smiling at Deane's surprise. "My, uh, informants—that's what you call them in both the CIA and linguistics, isn't it? Yes, well, my informants have told me all about this most remarkable *yanqui* who speaks the languages of my ancestors as if he belonged among them. You're a famous man in Yucatan, Doctor."

Deane shook his head. It was not unusual that Faranza's network of shady acquaintances in Merida knew various details of his life. He had been approached countless times by such men hoping to enlist him as a smuggler of various kinds of contraband: archeological treasures, drugs, secrets, weapons—he had lost track.

"I'm sure your friends also reported that I have refused repeatedly to help them smuggle their 'treasures' out of this country. I doubt if we have any business to transact, Faranza."

The giant Mayan stood abruptly, causing Deane to take a reflexive step backwards. Smiling innocently, Faranza raised his hands.

"You misjudge me, Doctor," he said in hurt tones. "I do not wish you to smuggle anything *out* of the country, I want you to take me *into* the country with you. I want to work with you in the Serpentine Mountains."

Caught completely off guard by Faranza's strange request, Deane could only reply, "Why?"

"Because I need the jade and serpentine of those mountains for my work," Faranza said. Then he added, with a sheepish grin, "and also because the customs police in Merida are watching me."

"What work?" Deane asked. "Besides smuggling stolen museum pieces out of Mexico, that is."

Faranza looked puzzled for a moment, then broke into roaring laughter. "Ho! Even you thought it was real, didn't you!" he bellowed. His voice echoed around the small room. Deane heard mumbled complaints from disturbed guests next door. "Admit it! You were fooled by my work, too!"

"Shhhh! Some of our neighbors are already in bed, Faranza. What are you talking about?"

"The sculpture!" he exclaimed, his whisper not much quieter than his bellow. "*My* sculpture! You thought it was Olmec. I have captured the style so well that it fooled even you, and you have studied it for years. Doctor, you make me very happy!"

"*You* sculpted that figure at the airport?" Deane's own voice was raised this time. Faranza, smiling, cautioned him with a finger to his lips.

"Remember our fellow guests at this most discriminating hotel," he whispered sarcastically. "You don't believe that I, Luis Faranza, could have done such delicate work with these paws, heh?" He thrust his large hands into Deane's face. "Here. I will show you!"

Faranza returned to the bed and reached down to pick up the canvas valise Deane had seen him carry. Unzipping the bag, the Mayan dumped its contents onto the sagging double bed's clean spread. Several tissue-wrapped objects tumbled onto the soft surface, along with the milky green statuette, still unwrapped, from the airport.

Deane moved hesitantly across the worn carpet to the bedside. Faranza lifted the figurine in his massive brown hands. Holding it to the light, he pointed to the figure's neck, just under the chin.

"Look closely and you will see Luis Faranza's signature mark. It appears as an 'equal' sign with a dot above it."

Deane took the statuette, marveling at its weight and polished smoothness. It was a perfect Olmec sculpture in every detail, unlike any he had ever seen in any museum, yet precise in style. Several scratches and gouges on its surface were caked with hardened red clay as if it had been buried for centuries. It was exactly what one would expect a genuine Olmec artifact to look like, except for a tiny detail below the chin. Just where Faranza had indicated, Deane saw two miniscule parallel lines with a pinpoint hole above them. They were so small, almost microscopic, that they were nearly invisible. In fact, it was only the same clay which filled the other scratches that made them detectable.

"Now, look at this one," said the Mayan, unwrapping another object. Looking, Deane saw a fetal-headed human figure, seated in a cross-legged posture, another common

Olmec motif. This too was a perfect example of the Olmec style, and it also had the dotted equal sign, but on one of its wrists rather than under the chin.

"And another," Faranza told him. The third was not a figurine, but a piece of serpentine tile which had a feline shape etched deeply in its mottled blue surface. The Mayan's finger was pointing to his 'signature' in one of the corners, on the dirt-encrusted rear side.

"The others have the same mark, I assure you," he told the astonished Deane. "I dislike having to disfigure my work with scars and mud, but my customers seem more willing to purchase pieces with 'grave dirt' and 'trowel marks' remaining on their surfaces. It makes them more 'authentic.' As you can see, I have a perverted sense of humor. I always apply the clay *after* I sign them so that my mark appears to be part of the original design, if it is noticed at all. By now, Faranza originals are in the hands of private collectors throughout the world, and have begun to reach the best museums by the donations of generous patrons who wish tax deductions."

Deane looked again at the three pieces in front of him. There was no doubt that the mark was identical on each item. Faranza had done an excellent job filling the other small grooves with 'original' clay, and he had even known enough to add fake scars made by archeological 'excavation.' Marveling at the big man's skill, Deane was certain that any expert would reach the same conclusion without having details of an archeological report. There were so many smuggled but genuine artifacts circulating in the world's antiquities market that no one would question the authenticity of these perfect "Olmec" sculptures. They would be worth hundreds of thousands of dollars on the private collector's markets.

"But now I have exhausted my supply of the same jade

and serpentine used by the Olmecs," added Faranza mournfully. "I need to make an expedition to the Tuxtla Mountains near Monte Azul, but the customs officials will want to know why I am there. If I am working with you, they would let me hunt for the minerals without question."

Deane was beginning to waver in his first reaction to Faranza. There was a kindred roguishness about the man that amused him, and the delicacy of his sculpture was proof of a very rare artistic talent. Still, he did not want to attract the interest of the Federal police.

"I have to report anyone I hire to the Mexican government, and there's no way I can justify paying you," he told the Mayan reluctantly, figuring that would end the matter.

But Faranza only smiled broadly. "You need someone who speaks Zoque, and my mother was pure Zoque from Kaktunque, near Monte Azul," he said, pleased at surprising Deane once again with his knowledge. "You have been asking for someone who speaks both Mayan and Zoque." Faranza tapped himself on his broad chest. "Now you have such a man for a guide and field assistant. One who is also an expert on Olmec sculpture. Pay me whatever the government will allow."

The offer was tempting. If Faranza really spoke Zoque, he could save months of work searching for a translator, who would, even then, probably be illiterate and would have to be trained. Plus it might be useful to have an assistant with family ties in the Monte Azul region.

Deane felt himself weakening. The big man intrigued him. He found himself liking him and—he had to admit—it would be lonely up in the mountains. Faranza could prove an amusing companion.

"Be here in the morning by nine," Deane told his new assistant and guide. "We have to find a second-hand truck."

"I know of one already, Steven!" Faranza exclaimed. "A government jeep was, uh, 'found' by a friend of mine. It has been repainted, and the serial numbers have been filed—"

"No!" interrupted Deane hastily. "We don't want a stolen truck! Just be here at nine!"

"Whatever you say," Faranza agreed with a shrug of his giant shoulders. He began stuffing the counterfeit Olmec sculptures back in his valise.

The last was the serpentine square, still lying in the middle of the sagging bed. The light gleaming on its etched surface drew Deane's attention to it, then he was caught and held by the unusual design. But before he could study it more closely, Faranza grabbed it and tossed it into the bulging canvas bag. With a wave, the sculptor left the room. As the door shut behind the Mayan, Deane could still see—in his mind's eye—the sea-green tile with its grotesquely beautiful etching—the snarling muzzle of a wild jaguar.

ARUCA

The afternoon rains had soaked Deane's thin denim clothes, but he didn't notice. He hadn't noticed much of anything during the walk from the Olmec ruins, a distance of nearly twenty miles from Kaktunque. His mind kept going over and over the incident until he felt physically weak and dizzy, and he was relieved to reach the village. Here, at least, was hard reality!

At the edge of the village he saw a boy, around nine years old, trying to drag his little sister inside their house.

"Hey, Bocarito!" Deane called through the downpour.

The boy paused, squinting into the rain until he recognized the *yanqui*, and waved.

"Has Don Luis Faranza returned from Monte Azul?" Deane shouted anxiously. He was tired, his shoulder ached from carrying the heavy canvas bag that contained his precious tape recorder. He suddenly began to worry that the rain might have damaged it. The waterproof case for the recorder was dented and battered after the two years he and Faranza had been in the field.

"It's due to leak," Deane thought glumly, "and this *would* be the time for it!"

"No, Don Esteban," the Indian child replied. "Perhaps he has moved away from Kaktunque. He has been gone a long time."

"Perhaps he has, Bocarito!" Deane grinned at the child, but his grin vanished as he entered the door to the two-room adobe shack on the edge of the village. He glanced anxiously at Faranza's work table in the corner just to be sure that the sculptor's counterfeit artifacts were still there.

The dozens of jade and serpentine statuettes, ritual axes, and other small sculptures were just as he had left them before daybreak, he saw. There were also several large carved columns called stelae, a huge Olmec head carved from a block of basalt, and even a can of red clay from the Tuxtla Mountains which Faranza used to coat his "discoveries" with a layer of ancient soil. Deane shook his head. Everything remained untouched. The sculptor had not done any work for the past three weeks.

"I wonder what's bothering Faranza," Deane thought, as he had been wondering for almost a month. "He's quit carving. He's been spending four days each week in Monte Azul, and he's become even more secretive than usual when he's here in Kaktunque."

The Mayan's strange behavior disturbed Deane. Though they had lived together nearly two years, he had never become close to the sculptor. Faranza was amiable, and they had a good working relationship.

Still, Deane was almost relieved Faranza was gone—at least tonight. He wanted to work alone for a while.

Deane carefully unpacked the tape recorder with its incredible recording from the Olmec temple. Checking the plastic inner liner, he found no leaks and sighed in relief. Leaving it on a table, he hastily dressed in dry clothes. Then, his hands shaking with eagerness, Deane lit the Coleman lantern and sat at his own work table to record his observations in his field diary.

After several minutes, the exhausted linguist stared at the limp page of his notebook. Reading it over, it sounded as unbelievable on paper as it had in his mind.

July 23, 1987

For the record, I am not hallucinating. Tired, excited, a little confused, perhaps, but definitely NOT INSANE!

AMAZING

Yet this morning, I saw an old Indian woman change into a jaguar, or something very much like a jaguar!

The air was clear at the ruins, visibility was perfect, and I was standing less than ten meters away. A deliberate illusion or trick would have been impossible to pull off, even if Aruca had known I was there. She was naked, her wrinkled brown skin outlined clearly against the gray limestone of the altar, and she was chanting in the same Zoque dialect as Miguel Trago.

Yellow and black fur appeared, first on her head, and then along her deformed arthritic spine just before she lurched forward onto the slab. I couldn't look away as the distinctive jaguar markings spread rapidly over the woman's writhing limbs and belly. Her chants changed to pained, inhuman grunts, then ripples of spotted fur and foreign muscles moved in waves over her distorted frame! In less than two minutes, I saw a large, healthy jaguar bound from the altar stone into the jungle!

Deane turned the page carefully to avoid tearing the damp paper. Wiping the sweat from his lower arm with his shirt, he continued his journal entry in a bold, black script.

The ground near the altar was covered with leaves and grass, making it impossible to confirm what I saw by tracks. I could only see Aruca's bare footprints approaching the ruins on the muddy trail, and I found a few smears of red clay on the Olmec altar. Fortunately, I was near enough to record the woman's vocal changes throughout the transformation. I now intend to digitalize the sounds in order to compare them with human speech ranges.

Deane glanced at the new paragraph, nodded to himself, and reached for the canvas-encased field recorder sitting on the camp table. Next to it was his portable computer, its power cables attached to the terminals of a heavy twelve-volt marine battery on the floor of the tent. The scientist flipped a switch on the console to check the amperage. Deane then connected the recorder to the computer's input jack. As soon as the digitalization program was loaded and ready, he pressed the playback button.

The first sounds were those of his own feet scuffling through the weeds and rubble of the overgrown Olmec temple. He remembered the predawn darkness as he had hidden himself behind the ancient limestone walls to record Aruca's morning prayers. The recorder was a delicate instrument, designed for the most demanding field use by professional linguists. Its sensitive heads heard and copied every sudden animal growl and bird call as the dank Mexican jungle awakened around the ancient ruins.

The decibel needle twitched as the computer's speech analysis program changed each nuance of sound to a sequence of ones and zeroes within the tiny machine's large memory. Deane's scalp prickled as he heard once more Aruca's soft footsteps padding toward the Olmec altar stone. Within moments, her eerie chant began. Leaning closer to the recorder, Deane listened intently to each syllable, trying to compare it in his mind to the curious dialect he had come so far to study.

Just as he was beginning to recognize some regular features of the strange speech sounds, Aruca's sing-song chant broke into more guttural utterances. In that instant, he was back in the ruins staring in horror at the furry creature that was neither human nor beast, but something from another reality! The inhuman vocalizations deteriorated to snarls and growls, while the nameless image in

Deane's brain crouched on its hind quarters and sprang into the sinister semi-darkness of the Mexican jungle. The linguist's mind cleared, erasing the disturbing memory, as the tape resumed its replay of the usual morning cries of hunters and their prey.

Flicking the switch on the tape recorder, Deane unplugged the jack from the computer. Then he entered a quick command on the keyboard and watched the small display screen for the results of the speech analysis. The three-inch diskette spun in its drive for a few seconds before the graph appeared on the monitor.

Deane squinted, using his hands to shade the display from the lantern's harsh glare as he studied the results. A gasp burst from his bearded lips while tears welled in his bloodshot eyes.

"Steven! The sun is up but you are not!"

Luis Faranza's loud voice and heavy hand on Deane's ankle ripped through the linguist's fabric of unpleasant dreams. At first, Deane felt a fleeting sense of relief. "It was a nightmare!" he thought. But when he saw the closed journal on the table next to the computer, he shuddered.

"Too much *agave* juice last night, heh? Or maybe old Aruca was too much woman for you!" Faranza snickered.

The sculptor's schoolboy humor usually just irritated Deane, but today it was intolerable, especially the disrespectful reference to the elderly Zoque woman.

"Shut up, Faranza! It's too early in the morning for your filthy jokes. Wait outside until I wake up and get my clothes on." Deane wondered groggily if the unscrupulous Faranza had read his notes, but dismissed the idea. He had never seen the Mayan read anything, and would have suspected he was illiterate had he not spoken such excellent English and Spanish.

"All right, Steven, but we must be at Monte Azul by noon if you wish to meet Miguel Trago. He is a *viejo,* an old man, and will not wait long. You've been wanting to record his words for many weeks—"

"I know!" snapped Deane, but Faranza was not to be sidetracked.

"It cost us seventy pesos to bring him to town!"

"You mean it cost me that much, Luis, and I'll bet at least twenty of those pesos are still in your damn pocket!"

The Mayan frowned, his dark lips protruding beneath a thin black moustache. "It is sad that you still do not trust me, Steven! When you first needed someone to talk in Zoque to these peasants, it was I who offered to help you. Have you forgotten my invaluable services to you in these past two years?"

Deane splashed water into his bleary eyes. Faranza threw him a towel and handed his employer a clean shirt.

"Invaluable services! You're a damned liar!" Deane snorted, relaxing and grinning as he buttoned the faded denim shirt. "You remember a few words of Zoque from your mother, maybe, but that's all."

"But it is odd," Deane thought to himself, "that the bits and pieces of Zoque Faranza speaks are difficult grammatical constructions; phrases only those totally familiar with the language would be likely to know. Yet Faranza swears now he doesn't remember it!"

Deane became so interested in considering this mystery that, for a moment, he forgot his other troubles.

Faranza screwed his brown face into a theatrical "hurt feelings" mask. "Once again, you insult me, my friend! You came to my country as little more than a schoolboy, wishing to learn about the splendors of my ancestors—the Olmec. It was I who arranged for you to live in their original homeland and who showed you the most hidden of

Olmec ruins. You will become famous in your country because of what Luis Faranza has taught you!"

Deane shook his head ruefully. It was true that Faranza had been a resourceful field assistant. Quite by accident, the sculptor had heard an old man speaking an unfamiliar form of Zoque in the marketplace several weeks before. Faranza later learned that an old Indian herbalist named Aruca spoke the same language when she said her prayers each morning. Deane's excitement was intense. From Faranza's account, he believed that the two elders were speaking an archaic form of Zoque, perhaps one similar to the same language spoken by the Olmec themselves! This could provide invaluable information about the Olmecs and their vanished civilization.

Enjoying playing detective, Faranza spied upon both Aruca and the old man. He learned that the old man's name was Miguel Trago, and that both he and the old woman, Aruca, lived in the highlands above Monte Azul. They were hermits, apparently. No one seemed to know where they came from, nor anything about their families. That was peculiar in a place where everyone was related in some way to everyone else.

"Perhaps you're right, Faranza," Deane admitted, watching a pleased smile spread across the man's face. "We could be on the verge of the most important discovery in Mesoamerican linguistics and archeology—a proven connection between the Olmec and Zoque civilizations! And I will see you get part of the credit!"

Nodding happily, Faranza hurried out the door, motioning impatiently for Deane to follow. The linguist came more slowly.

"Even more important," he thought with growing excitement, "will be my discovery of an archaic dialect which blended Olmec and Zoque phrases into a spell that

---

28

can change an old woman's frail, crippled body into that of a powerful jungle cat!"

"Steven!" came Faranza's warning voice.

Hastily Deane thrust his recorder, notebook and some extra tapes into his knapsack and started for the door behind Faranza. Then he stopped. On impulse, he grabbed the tape of Aruca's prayers and dropped the recording into his pack.

Monte Azul was more than twenty miles from Deane's base in the village of Kaktunque. The "road" up the mountain was nothing but a muddy trail, open only to the most rugged four-wheel or four-legged vehicles. The jeep Faranza had procured nearly two years before in Merida had developed transmission problems and was useless for such a journey. Luckily, the two burros the Mayan had scavenged for the day were healthy enough to withstand the rigorous trek. Deane and Faranza ambled into Monte Azul less than fifteen minutes after the arranged time to meet the old hermit, Miguel Trago.

"The cantina is there, by the stables," said Faranza, grinning at Deane's expression of abject misery as he climbed stiffly off the back of the burro.

"I see it," Deane mumbled, groaning and rubbing his aching buttocks. "I've got to stretch my legs. You go on inside. I'll take the animals to the stable and unpack my gear."

Faranza nodded without comment. He knew that Deane always preferred to handle the delicate recording equipment himself.

"I will order cool beer for you and tequila for the old man before I leave," he replied.

"Leave . . . where are you going?" Deane asked absently, his thoughts on his forthcoming interview.

"I have a . . . lady friend. . . ." Faranza said with a leer and a wink.

Deane nodded in sudden understanding. So that was the reason for Faranza's frequent trips to Monte Azul!

Dismounting, Faranza handed his burro's reins to Deane, then hurried onto the wooden porch of the saloon. Before Deane could offer to give him a few pesos for the drinks, the Mayan had disappeared.

Deane led the two burros to the stable, idly wondering what pretty girl had succumbed to Faranza's charms this time! It took him a while to find a boy to feed and water the animals, then he had to unpack his field recorder along with a notepad. He hoped Faranza was keeping Miguel Trago occupied so that the old man would not leave.

When Deane finally hurried into the dingy bar, he saw—to his disgust—that Faranza was not there. Deane looked around for the old man.

He found Miguel Trago sitting at a dirty table in an empty corner of the crude bar. He was an elderly peasant, whose mahogany skin was wrinkled and supple, like fine tanned leather.

"*Buenas tardes, Senor Trago,*" Deane greeted the old man in slow, deliberate Spanish, suspecting that the hermit probably knew very little of Mexico's national language. He was right. The peasant stared at him suspiciously. Deane switched immediately to the rural Zoque dialect.

"Forgive me for the delay, Don Miguel. I had to come a long way this morning to talk with you, and the road was very bad in this weather."

Trago's face brightened when he heard the more familiar language. The old man nodded solemnly, waiting for Deane's next words. The linguist had learned to appreciate the reticence of rural Indians. They seldom chatted idly with outsiders and seemed to prefer direct conversations.

"I've come to listen to your speech, Don Miguel," Deane said. "My helper, Faranza, told me that you speak an old form of Zoque, and I want to learn it. This box is a machine which will listen to your words and remember them for me."

Deane had experimented with many ways to explain a tape recorder to rural Indians. There were no words in Zoque or Mayan for the verb "record," but "remember" conveyed his intentions well enough to satisfy his sense of ethics. Deane disliked recording anyone's words without their knowledge as he had done with Aruca. If she had not disappeared, he would have tried to talk to her directly about what he heard her chanting.

"Why does a young man like yourself want to remember the words of an old shaman?" Miquel Trago asked. Deane smiled. The "shaman" was promising. Crudely translated, it meant "medicine man," and rural healers often knew more about traditional life and culture than anyone else in their communities.

"Because the old ways of the Zoque are almost lost," Deane answered, sitting down and switching on the machine. He glanced curiously at the old man as he did so, and for a moment experienced the uncanny feeling that he had seen Trago before, perhaps even talked with him! Almost angrily, Deane shook his head to clear it of such unscientific thoughts. The old man was like a hundred other old peasants, only this one spoke a language nearly lost in the modern world. The sense of *déja vu* passed quickly as Deane forced himself to concentrate on the archaic vowels and consonants of Trago's speech.

The interview proceeded slowly, because Trago had difficulty understanding Deane's more modern Zoque speech. Deane soon gathered that Trago really was a hermit, who had spent most of his solitary life in the caves above Monte Azul, scavenging the surrounding hills for small game and wild plant food. He came to town occasionally, he said, to trade herbs for sacks of meal and beans.

Once the conversation began to flow more comfortably, Deane tried to channel it toward the Indian's background. "Were you born near Monte Azul, in the Serpentine Mountains?" Trago answered the question immediately in the same ancient dialect Deane had come to study. But there were so many other unintelligible words mixed in that the scientist was positive some other dialect was blended with Zoque in Trago's speech.

"Pardon me? . . . Would you repeat that? . . . I didn't catch your meaning . . ." Deane's side of the interview was a record of his frustration with the unusual sounds.

Finally he gave up. Until he had time to study the recording, Deane knew he would not be able to understand more than the broadest gist of his interview with Trago, although the frequency of names in Trago's monologue made the American fairly sure that he was hearing about family details, geographic locales, and local gods.

". . . but Pagda never went to Mulcan before the ritual of corn and meat could be offered to Shutec, Lord of the Sky." It was while Trago was reciting names, apparently those of relatives, that Deane heard one he recognized.

". . . and lived at Talzok with my sister, Aruca—"

"Aruca!" Deane interrupted. He was bursting with excitement but wanted to hide it from the hermit. "Is this the same 'Aruca' who lives near here?" he asked more casually. "The old woman who collects medicine plants?"

The old Indian's watery eyes narrowed with caution. He seemed to be judging whether or not he could trust this foreigner.

Deane reached a decision. He would play the temple

recording for him.

"With your permission, Don Miguel, I want you to listen to something and tell me what you hear."

Miguel Trago stared at him suspiciously, but Deane was too excited to explain further. Fumbling in the pocket of the recorder's canvas case, he found the tape of Aruca's chant. When the cassette was set, he lowered the volume and motioned for Trago to lean closer to the speaker.

At the first syllable of the eerie prayer, Trago stiffened, an expression of total astonishment filling his withered face. As the chant continued, a look of horror clouded that of surprise, and the old hermit's shoulders began to tremble. Just as Aruca's voice started to change into the snarls of a jungle cat, Trago blurted a loud stream of unknown phrases in his ancient dialect. Deane could tell that they were words of anger from the expression on the old man's face, and hurriedly switched off the recorder to calm him.

It was too late. The docile old man had become a maniac! With a sweep of his arm, Trago knocked the delicate recorder from the table, hurling it against the tavern's adobe walls. Then he leapt to his feet. Screaming something in his strange language, he headed for the door.

"Wait! Just tell me what she is saying!" Deane cried, grabbing hold of Trago and trying to stop him. But the old hermit broke Deane's grip with surprising strength. Thrusting the young man aside, he ran for the door. Deane paused a moment to pick up his precious recorder and check it for damage, then he raced outside after the hermit.

Trago was gone. Vanished. Deane stared around in astonishment. The town of Monte Azul consisted of a single wide avenue with buildings extending on either side for only a few hundred yards. It was siesta hour, the street was deserted. Deane could see the entire village from the doorway of the cantina. The old hermit had disappeared.

"Trago! Don Trago!" Deane called loudly. Behind him, he heard the bartender and a few of his regular siesta clientele grumble about the rudeness of *yanquis.*

"What is it? What has happened, Steven?"

Deane turned to see Luis Faranza emerging from an alley behind the cantina. Near the back stairs, it was used by the tavern's bar women and their customers. The big Mayan was buckling his belt and his face was flushed with whatever vigorous pleasures he had been pursuing when he'd heard Deane shout.

"Miguel Trago left. Where would he go?" Deane demanded.

Faranza tilted his head toward the alley. "Back that way, toward the mountains. You'll never catch that old goat. What did you say to make him run?"

"I mentioned Aruca," Deane replied uneasily. "She's related to Trago in some way, apparently. I guess my questions about her upset him."

Faranza shook his head.

"No, Steven," he said cunningly. "That isn't all of the matter. You are hiding something from me. I heard the old one yelling. If you tell no one, no one can help you!"

"Let's go back to Kaktunque, Luis. I need to check the recorder for damage and then try to translate this dialect."

Deane and Faranza began the return trek to Kaktunque in silence, Deane brooding about the old hermit; Faranza—from the smile on his lips—thinking pleasanter thoughts. The burros plodded relentlessly along the muddy mountain trail, rocking their riders into a fatigued stupor. Deane caught himself napping several times and almost slipped from the saddle once or twice.

"So Monte Azul's where you've been spending your time!" he called ahead to Faranza, making idle conversation just to stay awake. The giant Mayan's huge figure was

34

ludicrous astride the small burro as he reined the animal in to let Deane amble alongside him.

"The women in Kaktunque are boring," he declared.

"You mean their husbands are getting smarter!" Deane retorted. "Anyway, you've gotten to be such a stranger in Kaktunque that little Boca asked me yesterday if you had moved away."

Faranza laughed but did not reply. Suddenly he kicked his burro, urging it forward, adding something lamely about the trail narrowing up ahead. Once more, Deane wondered what was wrong with the Mayan sculptor.

Deane had noticed Faranza becoming restless after they had been in Kaktunque for little more than a year. He had urged the sculptor repeatedly to take some time away from his work, perhaps visit Merida or Vera Cruz. But Faranza always refused. For the first half of their second year together, the Mayan seldom left Deane's side.

"I am your bodyguard," Faranza would say jokingly, but Deane had often wondered if the big man *were* joking. In vain Deane pointed out that he could take care of himself. Faranza was always with him, dogging his footsteps. This was also the sculptor's most industrious period. During those six months, Faranza had worked long hours, filling their hut with counterfeit Olmec pieces, each bearing the microscopic dotted equal sign which was Faranza's secret joke.

Then, perhaps a few months before, Faranza had begun absenting himself from Kaktunque for longer and longer periods. At first Deane actually welcomed the solitude. He had nearly finished his reports on the literacy study and was just getting ready to concentrate entirely upon his personal Olmec linguistics project when Faranza returned to Kaktunque one day, announcing his discovery of Aruca and Trago.

Thinking of Faranza's help in his project, Deane felt a pang of guilt. Perhaps Faranza was truly hurt that Deane didn't trust him. But the scientist did not want to say anything to anyone about Aruca's jaguar transformation.

"I have to be sure of my own sanity first," Deane said to himself to ease his conscience. "Maybe I just need to lie on the beach for a few weeks. I wouldn't be the first fieldworker to crack up!" But no! He had Aruca on tape! And he had Trago's strange reaction. He was suddenly eager to translate the old man's words. It might give him a clue. . . . It might prove he wasn't going crazy!

Night had fallen by the time they reached Kaktunque. Deane sent Faranza into the village to return the burros and find some late supper for them both. As soon as the big man left, Deane pulled out his journal and wrote down a description of the interview with Miguel Trago, including as much as he could remember about the old man's reaction to the recording of Aruca's chant. Satisfied that the account was complete, Deane then checked the charge on the field computer and connected the recorder to it. Within minutes, the entire dialogue with the old hermit had been digitalized and read into the memory of the machine.

Using a special analysis program which counted the occurrences of similar speech fragments, Deane began dividing Trago's sentences into individual phrases and words, separating those he recognized from those he did not. Soon, the screen filled with familiar phonetic symbols, arranged in their most likely patterns of meaning. Deane studied the sequences until he started recognizing some regular clusters of consonant and vowel sounds among the unknown phrases. It was like breaking a code.

Then, after an hour of juggling his data, the key to the "code" suddenly appeared on Deane's screen. With mounting excitement, he saw that some of the terms were identical to a remote but known dialect, except for some regular substitutions of certain sounds! Both Miguel Trago and Aruca seemed to be speaking an old form of Zoque, sprinkled with some words from another Indian language called Huastec, usually spoken much farther north!

Intrigued with his discovery, Deane hastily rummaged through his library of diskettes until he found the one with the Huastec dialect he remembered.

Deane proceeded carefully, using the computer to experiment with other substitutions. It worked! Slowly he began building a list of vocabulary words in the new dialect he had apparently discovered. The patterns emerged gradually, until Deane began to recognize systems of suffixes and prefixes which were unlike anything in either Zoque or Huastec. He could now attempt a translation of Aruca's chant!

Hands trembling with excitement and anxiety, Deane loaded the "prayer" into memory and entered the translation command. Almost instantly, the computer's version of Aruca's mystical chant appeared on the small screen:

```
#####CALL##### RAIN ##### TODAY
HUNT ##### FROGS NOT ###### PRIEST-
SISTER## GOD ##### NOT DEAD NOT DIE NOW
################?????????????????????????
?????????????????????????????????????????

# = UNTRANSLATABLE HUMAN SPEECH
? = NOT HUMAN SPEECH

TRANSLATION COMPLETE.
DO ANOTHER (Y/N)? _____
```

Lacking a printer, Deane copied the computer's data exactly from the screen into his notebook and then pressed the "N" key to exit from the translation program. The young scientist read the cryptic message several times, comparing it to the notes he had made of the translated interview with Trago, trying to piece together this puzzle.

The phrase the computer translated as "PRIEST-SISTER" in Aruca's chant was absent from Miguel's conversation, although the portion it recognized as "SISTER" appeared several times. Just before Aruca's name was mentioned in Trago's dialogue, among a list of other female names, the computer had translated a string of sounds as ". . . SISTER. . . ." The hermit must have been referring to the old woman as a "sister" of some kind! So they *were* related!

The phrase rendered as "JAGUAR" in Aruca's chant was very similar to all known Mayan names for the beautiful jungle cat, differing only in one vowel sound. This probably meant that they stemmed from a common ancient form, perhaps one used by the pre-Mayan Olmecs!

Deane was still studying various alternative translations on the screen when he heard Faranza coming up the road, singing. With an exhausted sigh, Deane copied all of the analysis from the machine's memory onto the diskette and removed it from its drive. He did not want the Mayan to see what he had been working on, so he grabbed a game diskette from the pile of programs and hurriedly thrust it into the console.

He noticed absently that it was one called "Polaris," a game based upon a futuristic setting in Antarctica after a nuclear holocaust. It seemed to be taking a long time for the opening screen to appear. Too long. Deane drummed his fingers on the table nervously. He wanted to look as if he had been innocently absorbed in the game when Faranza entered.

"The battery must be growing weak," he thought irritably. When the opening screen finally did appear, the characters flickered in an unusual way, as if something was wrong with the program. Deane stared at it in astonishment. This was certainly not "Polaris!"

JAGUAR! JAGUAR! JAGUAR! DEANE! STEVEN! YOU MUST PLAY POLARISJAGUAR! AT ONE OF THE FOLLOWING LEVELS STEVEN DEANE:

1. NOVICE 2. ADVANCED 3. EXPERT

SELECT YOUR LEVEL OF PLAY VERY CAREFULLY BECAUSE YOU WILL NEVER BE ABLE TO RETURN TO THIS PAGE OF THE PROGRAM. IF YOU NEED HELP MAKING THIS PERMANENT DECISION, ENTER THE WORD "HELP" INSTEAD OF A LEVEL.

LEVEL SELECTED: _____

Stunned, Deane's gaze focused on the single word that had dominated his thoughts so completely for the past two days: JAGUAR! *And the program was using his name!*

"What in hell . . .?"

"What is it?" asked Faranza, who was just entering the hut. "Is something wrong with your computer?"

"I'm not sure," Deane answered. "Come look!"

His fingers flew over the keyboard, entering the word HELP just as the sculptor joined him at the table. In only a few seconds, the opening menu was replaced by an even stranger set of instructions:

HELP SCREEN

SELECT 'NOVICE' IF YOU HAVE NEVER PLAYED THIS GAME BEFORE. IT IS EASIER TO 'WIN' AT THE NOVICE LEVEL BECAUSE THE SOLUTIONS ARE SIMPLER AND PHYSICAL.

SELECT 'ADVANCED' IF YOU FEEL THAT YOU ARE READY TO ANSWER MORE DIFFICULT QUESTIONS—BE READY TO FACE CONFUSION.

SELECT 'EXPERT' ONLY IF YOU ARE CONFIDENT THAT YOUR SANITY IS STRONG ENOUGH TO HANDLE LARGER MYSTERIES.

YOU WILL 'WIN' THIS 'GAME' ONLY WHEN YOU UNDERSTAND EVERYTHING THAT IS HAPPENING AT ANY MOMENT. YOU WILL KNOW WHEN YOU HAVE REACHED THE END

The strange "HELP" messages remained on the screen for a few seconds, then were replaced by a slightly changed menu. Deane and Faranza stared at the monitor, hypnotized by the blinking green lights.

If you were in Steven Deane's place right now, which level would you select? Remember your choice and continue reading on the next page.

THE GAME BEGINS . . .

"What does that mean, Steven?" Faranza asked, leaning over Deane's shoulder to peer at the strange message on the screen. "How does it know your name?"

"I'm not sure, but I intend to find out!"

"Well, do it without me. I don't like to play with a machine who knows my name. I will sculpt and think of the fun *I* have with my games in Monte Azul while you and your machine have fun together."

Deane grabbed Faranza's arm as the man turned away.

"Wait, Luis! This isn't a game! It's not supposed to be doing this! Let's see what happens." He jabbed a key, at the same time pulling the reluctant guide closer to the table. Almost immediately, the menu of game options vanished. It was replaced by a pulsating dot in the center of the small screen—a bright *red* dot.

"That's impossible!" Deane gasped. "This isn't a color monitor!"

"What is a monitor?" asked Faranza, tensing as he felt Deane's growing fear and confusion.

"The screen. A monitor's like a . . . a TV screen! I use it to see the computer's output. Monitors come in black and white or color, just like regular television sets, and this one's black and white."

"But if it's not a color set, how can that blinking dot be red?" Faranza frowned.

"That's why I said it's impossible, Luis! Whatever has happened to this game program is really . . ."

Deane's babbling was interrupted suddenly by a low whine from somewhere inside the computer. It seemed to be a wavering, shifting frequency that penetrated his skull, searching his brain for a matching wavelength. Panic gripped Deane as he realized he could not tear his attention away from the red dot and the hypnotic whine. The last images Deane had were of Faranza's white-knuckled fingers gripping his arm and the pulsating red glow. . . .

Darkness! Suddenly Deane realized he was sitting in a darkened room. The glare of the camp lantern was gone! The only light came from the soft greenish glow of the computer's monitor. Deane looked quickly around. He could see his hands, as well as the keyboard and console, in front of him on the rough table. Then he noticed that Faranza's fingers had loosened their grip. The Mayan was now lying in a crumpled heap beside Deane's chair!

Forcing himself to remain calm, Deane rose shakily from his chair and knelt beside the sculptor's body. He felt Faranza's pulse and respiration and was relieved to note the man's heartbeat, though slow, was strong. Faranza's breathing was very shallow, like that of a man in a trance.

"Hypnotized!" Deane thought, shaken.

"Luis! Can you hear me?" Deane shook his companion's shoulders and head, but the Mayan remained in his hypnotic trance on the damp stone floor.

Stone! The floor of their adobe hut was baked clay!

Deane glanced quickly around, feeling a chill of fear convulse his body. The one-room shack was gone! The adobe walls and clay floor had been replaced by perfectly smooth rock walls! Everything had changed except for the table, chair, and computer—and themselves! Deane's cot, his trunk, the lantern, Faranza's sculpting table and his sculptures, everything else had disappeared!

Leaping to his feet, Deane groped desperately at his pockets, more from a desire to test his reality and wakefulness than to check their contents. His fingers felt the reassuring familiar bulges of his pen, notebook, wallet, pocket knife, Bic lighter, and a few pesos. Glancing down at his body, he saw that nothing had changed about his clothes.

"What is happening!" Deane felt a shriek of panic rise up in his throat, then firmly pulled himself together.

"I must stay calm!" he told himself. "There's a logical explanation."

Taking a deep breath, he turned back to the table and examined the computer. The small machine was still on, its greenish light the only thing illuminating the surroundings. The computer's power cable still snaked over the edge of the table. Deane forced his trembling hands to find his Bic lighter and flicked it on after several tries. Holding it down near the floor, he could see that the heavy plastic umbilicus had remained connected to the marine battery.

"My research!"

Suddenly remembering his canvas field bag with its precious diskettes, Deane crawled under the table and pawed around desperately. No use. He groaned in despair. His only records of the entire field trip were gone!

Then he remembered the journal.

"At least I have the raw field notes," he thought, trying to ease his bitter pain. "I can duplicate the analysis." The heat of the Bic reminded him that the lighter was still on and that he might need to conserve whatever butane was left. Extinguishing the flame, he stood up and reached his hand out to retrieve the journal. It had been sitting beside the computer . . .

But even before he touched the bare table, he knew that the spiral notebook was not going to be there. Desperately, Deane lifted the computer console and keyboard. The journal had vanished along with everything else except—

"Except what I was touching!" he exclaimed aloud. The sudden sound of his own voice echoed in the rock chamber.

"What are you saying, Steven?" Faranza's muffled and

dazed voice from the floor startled him. The husky Mayan seemed to be recovering from the mysterious hypnotic effects of the computer program.

"What has happened? What is this place?" the sculptor exclaimed as he rose shakily to his feet and stared around.

"I guess we both blacked out when that light and hum started coming from the computer," Deane answered, trying to keep his voice from cracking with tension. "I woke up just a few minutes ago and found you on the floor."

"But where are we?" Faranza persisted, looking at Deane expectantly.

"I don't know!" Deane practically yelled, then got a grip on himself again. He continued more calmly. "All I know is that my diskettes and notes are gone. I haven't had time to look around."

"But how did all of this happen?" the Mayan demanded, as if certain Deane were responsible. "I don't remember anything."

"I keep telling you, I don't know!" Deane sighed wearily. "All I remember is the screen going blank as soon I touched the key. Then we saw the red light. It must have hypnotized us, or something like that. I seem to remember a whining sound. . . ."

"Yes!" Faranza exclaimed. "It was like the sound of my own heartbeat!"

"That's it—our heartbeats!" Deane paused to think. "I don't know if our internal rhythms changed to match it or if it matched them, but that might be the answer to how we were hypnotized. Anyhow, while we were in the trance, everything disappeared except what I was touching, including you. Look—the chair, the table, and the computer—even the battery connected by a cable to the machine!"

Faranza glanced at it fearfully. "Maybe this is a dream,"

---

he muttered. Suddenly he whirled away from the table and started pounding on the walls of the chamber, first with his palms and then with his fists. Shivering, he backed off. "It's solid rock," he murmured, rubbing his bruised knuckles.

"It looks like limestone, Luis," Deane said coldly, wondering what he would do if Faranza gave way to the same panicking feelings he himself was fighting. He tried to sound reassuring. "I think we're in a cavern of some kind. Look"—he pointed—"there's a tunnel or a door over to your left, on the other side of the room."

Just beyond the dim light of the monitor, a dark corridor exited the cave. Cave? Well, not quite.

"It's not a natural cave," Deane thought. "These walls have been cut and polished in the shape of a perfect cube! Nature didn't do this. But who did?"

"You are right!" Faranza sounded more cheerful now that he had found—apparently—a way out. "Let us explore."

"You stay here." Clutching the butane lighter, Deane crossed to the opening and stepped through it into a dense blackness. Looking around, he saw he was in a narrow corridor of stone. He walked cautiously ahead and the greenish light of the monitor behind him faded. Deane thrust the Bic lighter forward and thumbed the wheel. The bright gas flame glared against the walls of the tight passage, revealing only minute cracks in the smooth limestone rock walls for an unknown distance ahead.

"What do you see?" whispered Faranza. "Does it lead outside?"

Switching off the lighter's flame, Deane turned back, only to find Faranza's hulking figure blocked the meager light from the computer. He couldn't see a thing!

"Get back inside the room so I can see how to get out of

here," Deane snapped nervously. Faranza's apparent anxiety was just one more problem to handle when all he wanted to do was sit somewhere in peace and quiet and try to figure out what had happened!

"Someone has tampered with the computer program in some unknown manner," he thought. "But why? To steal my notes and diskettes? But how? No computer technology I have heard of could do what has been done to us! Whoever has engineered this elaborate kidnapping must understand computers far better than I do! Maybe by running the program again—"

"Look, Steven! A pot of oil!"

Faranza handed him a small clay lamp, filled with some kind of sour animal fat. It had a cloth wick floating in the thick grease and spilling over the vessel's side.

"A lamp!" Deane exclaimed. "Where did you find it?"

"On the floor, next to the entrance to the corridor."

"Great!" Deane mopped his sweating face. "We can turn off the computer and save its battery. We're going to need it to study the program that got us here."

Deane lit the cloth wick with his lighter. It spluttered and smoked, but finally began to burn with an acrid odor. Placing the lamp down on the table beside him, he sat in the chair in front of the console keyboard.

"Don't touch it, Steven!" warned Faranza. "That machine is possessed, and it will hypnotize us again. You must unplug it—quickly!"

"Possessed!" Deane snorted. "Just be quiet and let me think about this!"

Deane saw Faranza's hurt expression, but he had no patience left to deal with the frightened sculptor. It had just occurred to him that whatever program had been used to hypnotize them might still reside in the computer's temporary RAM memory. If so, perhaps he could analyze it to discover how the program had been altered!

"I've got to get the operating system back in control of the machine without resetting the memory," he mumbled to himself. "If I reset the console or cut it off, anything in the machine's memory circuits will be erased and we may never be able to know who did this to us, or how, or why."

After a moment or two, Deane leaned forward and gingerly pressed first the CONTROL key and then the C. Under normal circumstances, that sequence would result in a "warm" reset, restoring the operating system without disturbing the memory. But these circumstances were hardly normal! When the console's drives clicked, Deane covered his face in case the hypnotic glow returned. When he heard the normal sound of a diskette whirring in its drive, he nearly sobbed in relief. There was a softer click, then silence. Peering through his fingers at the monitor, Deane saw only the familiar A with the square cursor blinking next to it—signs that the operating system was in control of the console.

He then punched in the simple command, SAVE MEM. That should copy everything in the temporary memory onto the game diskette already in the drive.

There was the familiar, reassuring whir, then the computer's drive stopped after several seconds, and the A reappeared. His hand shaking, Deane pressed a D to view the diskette directory. There it was! Safely recorded: MEMCOPY—94K. The directory also listed the original game program, POLARIS.EXE, along with several other files which were probably separate data and help programs for the game.

Satisfied that he could now study the program under safer conditions, he quickly flicked the power switch on the console to conserve the dwindling power of the battery. The green glow from the monitor died.

"Is it safe?" asked Faranza.

Deane nodded as he removed the diskette from its drive. "The program that caused us both to black out is right here on this disk," he told the sculptor. "As soon as we have time, I'll look at it more closely. But first I want to get this cable off the battery so that it doesn't damage the circuits."

Kneeling on the rock floor, Deane disconnected the cable from the heavy battery and, as a safety precaution, he coiled the plastic cable tightly and hid it beneath some loose stones that had apparently fallen from the ceiling near the back wall. Then, reaching in his back pocket, he found a handkerchief and spread it on top of the table. He placed the precious diskette carefully in the middle of the white cloth and doubled its edges over the plastic square. It did not offer much protection, but it was all he had.

"How long do you think we were unconscious?" Faranza asked as Deane placed the wrapped diskette next to the cable in the cache of rubble by the wall.

"I don't know," Deane answered, thinking about it for the first time. "Let's see . . . it was almost midnight when that hypnosis program or whatever it was took control of us. I'm hungry but not starving, so I doubt if we've been in a trance longer than a day. I feel like I've just had a good night's sleep and I'm ready for breakfast."

Faranza nodded and patted his stomach. "I agree with you, Steven. Let's leave this place and find the nearest cafeteria. Perhaps there's one just down that passage." Thoughts of food seemed to have replaced Faranza's fear—either that or he was determined to hide it.

"I'm beginning to wish we had the rifle," said Deane. They used a .22 pump to shoot small game and rodents around their house, but the rifle had vanished with everything else. Picking up the small lamp, Deane headed for the opening, with Faranza sticking close behind him.

The corridor was much longer than Deane had guessed, and it cut straight through the limestone cavern for more than fifty feet. Then it ended.

"We're sealed up in this place! Locked in! It's a prison—" Faranza began to whimper and wring his hands.

"Shut up!" Deane ordered savagely, holding up the lamp to see better.

Faranza subsided, and Deane began to inspect the wall in front of them. He drew a deep breath.

"Look," he said to Faranza, "we're not sealed in. It's a slab of limestone like the tunnel walls all right, but—see? It's been precisely cut to fit inside the opening. It's like a— a plug. The edges of the slab are purposefully left jagged, probably designed to disguise the tunnel entrance leading to the chamber. I wonder why—"

Deane stopped talking and held the lamp closer to the slab. A bright metal ring protruded from the stone. Deane almost giggled; it looked for all the world like a doorknocker! He reached out to touch it with his free hand. The metal had a strange texture and weight. It was lighter than aluminum, yet somehow felt more solid in his palm. He pulled, but nothing happened.

"Let me try," whispered Faranza.

Deane spread himself against the wall of the narrow passage, watching as Faranza's huge fist closed around the metal rung. He saw the sculptor's powerful arm muscles bulge in the lamplight as he strained against the weight of the stone portal.

"Help me!" Faranza gasped. "I think it moved a little!"

Deane reached for the loop to add his strength to the Mayan's just as Faranza was shifting his position to get better leverage. Deane tripped over Faranza's big feet and stumbled against the sculptor's side, causing him to jerk on the metal ring. There was a sharp metallic click, the massive stone door shuddered, and a streak of red light appeared around the jagged edge of the portal.

"It locks . . . from the inside!" exclaimed Faranza in an astonished whisper, examining the ring.

"Funny kind of prison, wouldn't you say?" Deane muttered, eyeing the open doorway suspiciously.

"What's that light?" Faranza demanded, looking at Deane expectantly once again.

The light reminded Deane of a red neon sign blinking slowly and steadily from the other side of the slab. Counting the rhythmic pulses, he found they were about four seconds apart, without varying.

"Maybe it's that cafe you were hoping to find," he told Faranza. The big Mayan gave him a sickly grin that faded rapidly. "Well, there's only one way to find out," Deane added. Bracing himself, he pushed on the stone door at its edges. Surprisingly, the slab slid forward very easily, as if it were hinged and oiled. Red light flooded the tunnel and now he could see that the outer surface of the door sloped irregularly to the floor of the passage so that the slab resembled a natural cavern wall. Its uneven edges overlapped the opening so that it would be virtually impossible to detect the hidden chamber from the outside.

The slab had parted just enough for Deane to peer around its rough edge into the room beyond. He blinked in astonishment. He was looking at a wall made of glowing red mist that flashed bright and then dim with the regularity of a neon sign! Peering at it closely, Deane saw that the wall seemed transparent in spots, especially at the low points of its throbbing cycle of rhythmic flashes. It gave the appearance of an undulating barrier of lighted red gel. Then he gulped and drew back.

"What do you see?" Faranza asked impatiently.

"Quiet!" Deane hissed. "Someone's coming!"

Cautiously, Deane looked back around the rock slab, while Faranza dropped to his knees and squeezed his cheek against the wall to see what Deane was watching.

Beyond the wall of red mists, two strangely attired men stood behind a massive flat-topped boulder only several feet away from the lighted barrier. They were whispering together, and neither seemed to pay the least bit of attention to the curiously glowing wall.

"A costume party!" Faranza snickered. Deane nudged him with his foot.

The fatter of the two men wore an elaborate, feathered headdress and a woven loincloth. The other wore the same type of loincloth, but lacked the headdress. His bald scalp gleamed in the flashes of red light from the transparent wall. Both men were naked from the waist up, their upper bodies were painted with designs Deane did not recognize.

"This is no party! I think they're priests," Deane whispered. "That flat boulder's probably some sort of altar."

Now that Deane's eyes were accustomed to the pulsating light, he could see the cave chamber beyond the altar. It was a spacious cavern, with both small and large stalagmites protruding from the rock floor like teeth.

"They must be preparing for a ritual of some kind," Deane muttered, watching as the priest with the headdress lit torches around the chamber and stacked fresh cornstalks on the altar. The bald man did nothing but issue terse instructions to the other, who was obviously an inferior cleric of whatever strange gods they served.

Faranza started to ask something, but Deane nudged him into silence again. He had suddenly realized he could understand some of what the two men were saying! It was a form of Zoque-Huastec, the same ancient dialect spoken by Aruca and Trago.

51

"Are the warriors in the outer room, Cizin?" the junior priest was asking.

"Yes!" hissed his bald companion. "And they grow impatient! If Shutec does not appear to them this time, they will leave and take the meat with them. These cursed primitives do not revere our gods unless they see them."

"The altar is almost ready, my lord," said the underling. "You can don the sacred mask."

"Well, give it to me, you fool!" snapped the senior priest. "It is far too heavy to wear more than a few moments at a time."

Deane knelt down beside Faranza. "Have you ever heard of a god called Shutec?"

Faranza frowned. "What are they saying?" he asked.

"They're preparing for some kind of ritual for some warriors who are waiting outside," answered Deane. "They said something I don't understand about 'primitives' and gods. I think they plan to impersonate their own gods for these warriors, whoever they are. The skinny one has some kind of 'sacred mask' and he mentioned the name Shutec. Isn't that the ancient Mayan god of fire?"

"Yes," agreed Faranza, "but some legends say that Shutec is much older than the Maya, that they borrowed his name from the Olmec's most powerful deity."

Deane twisted his head to spy on the priests' preparations. The bald man was lacing a heavy disk over his head. It was a baked clay mask with a sunburst shape modeled on its outer surface. When it was in place, the lanky priest staggered under its weight.

"Let the barbarians in, Enul," he mumbled in a hollow voice muffled by the mask.

"Shutec, Lord of Fire!" stuttered his obviously dim-witted cleric, falling to his knees beside the altar.

"Get up, fool! You helped me put the mask on! Am I a

god? Go to the outer chamber and admit them before I am crushed beneath this thing!"

The masked cleric stumbled behind the altar while his rotund subordinate waddled among the limestone pillars toward the opposite end of the cave. Deane ducked away from the crack and motioned for Faranza to lean closer.

"One of them has gone to bring the warriors," he told the Mayan. "There's no other way out of here, so I think we ought to stay put until we know what's going on. I guess they think that red wall's just part of the cave. They don't even look at it."

Faranza nodded his agreement just as they heard the sound of many feet and voices echoing in the cavern. Both men hurriedly crammed their faces against the wall to watch the next scene in the strange drama unfolding outside the hidden portal.

The priest with the mask had crouched down behind the altar where he could not be seen from the cavern. At least a dozen men wearing round rawhide helmets and armed with black-tipped spears entered the large chamber, led by Enul, and more were following them. It was impossible to see all of them through the narrow slit, but Deane could hear the scraping of their feet and their echoing murmurs. The fat priest stood in front of the altar with his arms raised over his feathered head.

"Come to the altar of Shutec, men of Huasta!" shouted the fat priest. His feathered headdress quivered in the pulsating light as he faced the throng of primitive spearmen. The warriors mumbled in nervous voices as they crowded closer to the altar. But they weren't watching the priest.

"They're afraid of the red wall behind the priests," Deane whispered to Faranza. "They can't take their eyes off it."

When the helmeted fighters had all packed the space in

53

front of the great stone, their voices became louder.

"Where is this god of yours, Zoque slave?" one of the warriors called.

"Show us the god or we'll force you to give us the corn without the meat!" yelled another.

"Yes! Take the corn!"

Trembling visibly, the fat priest reached behind his back to the altar for an ear of corn. Raising it in his hand, he flung it straight into the pulsating red wall!

There was a blinding flare of pink light when the small cob struck the mysterious barrier. Until then, Deane had imagined the wall might be some kind of energy shield guarding the secret chamber. He expected the ear of corn to disintegrate or burn up. Then he saw the same cob lying unharmed and unchanged on the floor in front of them!

The corn appeared unchanged, but the wall itself was now filled with swirling dark-edged clouds of a thick red mist. It was so thick, in fact, that Deane could no longer see the priests or the warriors through it. But he realized something had happened because the warrior's voices all stopped abruptly.

Then he knew! "Shutec" had appeared! The fat priest had tossed the corncob into the wall to divert the warriors' attention while the "god" made his appearance from behind the altar.

Within a minute or two, the swirling mists settled and Deane could see through the barrier again. "Shutec" was standing behind the black altar, his masked figure framed by the flashing red wall. He held both hands high above his head and chanted in the ancient blend of Zoque and Huastecan. The fat priest had disappeared.

The primitive stage illusion must be effective, thought Deane, because the throng of fighters had become suddenly still, captivated by the highpriest's muffled voice.

"I, Shutec, Lord of Fire and Ruler of the Wall of Mists, have summoned you, Men of Huasta, to remind you of your obligations. The green corn is here, waiting to be sanctified with the blood of your beasts!"

"Shutec" stopped his muffled chant and pointed to the back of the ritual cavern. The warriors near the altar turned to watch something beyond Deane's view. Then he saw the fat Enul approaching the altar, walking in front of two warriors, who carried a huge carcass of some unknown beast between them on a sagging pole. It resembled an ungutted hog, but with a strange, elongated snout.

"A tapir!" Deane gasped when he finally recognized the beast. "Where could they have found that animal?" Even the small Central American tapir had virtually disappeared from Mexican jungles. Yet these men had apparently just killed one with their spears!

When the small procession reached the altar, "Shutec" issued another terse command. The two muscular soldiers heaved the bloody carcass onto the altar beside the stack of cornstalks. Then they moved back into the first rank of their fellow warriors squatting in front of the large stone.

"Shutec" raised a single hand high above his head. In the strobe effect of the lighted wall's rhythmic pulses, the obsidian dagger in his fist seemed frozen like individual frames of a rose-tinted movie film.

Then the dagger of black glass plunged into the tapir's carcass at least ten times in rapid succession. The highpriest disguised as a god slashed the animal's chest cavity, allowing its dark fresh blood to gush onto the pile of green stalks. The murmurs from the armed spectators grew louder and more excited with each thrust. But Deane could see the highpriest's slender legs wobble slightly, and guessed that the man was reeling beneath the great weight of the ceremonial mask. His stout assistant saw him stumble and rushed forward.

"The corn of the Zoque farmers has been consecrated by the blood of the Huasta hunters!" Enul announced.

The highpriest summoned what strength he had left and raised his hands again. Just as the audience shielded their faces, the fat Enul pitched another ear of corn into the pulsating wall. As before, it passed through the radiant barrier and landed on the floor in front of the secret door. Once again, too, there was a noiseless flash of tinted light and a sudden thickening of the mists floating in the wall. For several minutes, it was too opaque for Deane and Faranza to see the other side.

As it began to clear, they saw that the warriors were leaving the cavern in a rush, carrying large armloads of the bloody cornstalks. Only the tapir's carcass remained on the altar, still draining its dark fluids over the edges.

Enul watched the warriors scurry from the cavern with the corn they had purchased with their meat, while his master squatted on the floor with the clay mask resting against the side of the hewn boulder. The highpriest's face was livid and sweating, perhaps as much from fear as from exhaustion, Deane thought. If the warriors who had traded the meat for a few stalks of corn knew that the "god" who had demanded the swap was this balding cleric, their knives and spears would have a new target.

"Have they gone?" the highpriest whispered.

"Yes, but they are still in the outer chamber, Cizin," replied Enul. "We should wait until they have left the caves."

Deane was beginning to understand the Zoque-Huastec dialect more readily. It was becoming easy for him to distinguish between words and to guess at the unfamiliar ones. He was puzzled by something very peculiar—the total absence of borrowed words from Spanish, or even from Mayan! It was unthinkable to hear a "pure" Indian language in modern Mexico. Yet, he had just witnessed an ancient ritual between hunters and farmers which had been conducted in a mixture of two completely aboriginal dialects, the same language he had heard spoken by Aruca and Trago! He was beginning to put two and two together—and he wasn't at all sure he liked the answer!

"Who are these strange people?" Faranza whispered, seeing Deane's pale face. "Are they the ones who brought us here? What is wrong?"

Deane pushed himself away from the cracked doorway and beckoned for Faranza to follow him a few feet away from the end of the tunnel.

"Here's the way I see it, Luis," Deane began in a whisper. "Judging from the language those Indians were speaking and their costumes, it may have something to do with those Olmec ruins you found. I was convinced these guys just belonged to some kind of nativistic cult until . . . until they brought the dead tapir into the cave."

"What do you think now?" the Mayan pressed.

Deane looked past Faranza at the crevice of the secret door. His training as a scientist was making it difficult to answer the sculptor's question because his only proof lay on the other side of the flickering red wall. Finally he turned and leaned closer to Faranza's sweaty face.

"The best possible theory is that we've actually traveled back in time, Luis!" he murmured.

The Mayan regarded Deane dubiously, then shook his head. "Time travel? I thought you said it was a 'possible' theory! How could such a thing have happened?"

"I can't answer that yet," admitted Deane helplessly. "But, look at the evidence! Those people out there are speaking a pure, aboriginal Indian language. I'm absolutely sure of it! And that large tapir is extinct throughout

Central America! This is some kind of strange blend of past and future!"

Faranza was quiet for a moment. Then he furrowed his thick eyebrows and waved toward the cavern. "Just who do you think those people are then?"

"Didn't you see their helmets?" asked Deane. "You should have recognized them before I did, because you've just finished sculpting one. They're Olmec!"

Once more, Deane could see clearly in his mind the massive stone heads which had become accepted as the most obvious markers of the Olmec culture. The huge monuments bore the faces of ancient kings, each with thick lips and heavy jowls, very much like Faranza's. More to the point, each of the great heads of basalt wore a rounded helmet like those of the warriors in the cavern.

Faranza's face stiffened at Deane's mention of the helmets. He seemed angry at himself for having missed such an obvious clue to a sculptor's eye. "Why did you say it's a blend of the past with the future? I saw nothing futuristic about that ritual!"

Deane smiled as he pointed toward the chamber with the computer. "This tunnel and that cubicle have been cut perfectly from solid rock, Luis! I don't know of any tool capable of this kind of precision cutting without leaving scars on the walls. Also, the metal on that door latch is like no other metal I've ever seen, and—remember—you said yourself, it was locked from the inside!"

Faranza listened to Deane's explanation in silence, then he frowned. "So how did we get here?" he asked carefully.

"I'm not sure, but it has something to do with that tampered computer program. If we can find out who monkeyed with it, we'll probably learn how it was done." Deane also suspected Aruca and Trago were somehow involved in their mysterious teleportation, but it was only

58

a gut feeling. Besides, he was still unwilling to tell Faranza about the woman's transformation into a jaguar.

"What is that wall of lighted mists out there?" Faranza sneered. "Have you thought of a theory for that, too?" The sculptor sounded almost hostile, as if he resented Deane's logical though incredible explanation.

Deane sighed. "I have no idea, unless it's merely an optical illusion of some kind. These cavern walls are filled with pieces of jade and other crystals. It's possible that the reflections of the torches focus somehow on that particular spot. It doesn't seem to have any substance, although that misty stuff rises whenever it's disturbed. Whatever it is, it didn't hurt those corncobs, and I doubt if it would bother us if we went through it."

"What makes it blink?" pursued Faranza, glancing back at it dubiously. "Do you think it could be radioactive?"

"It's possible." Deane shrugged. "There's no way to know. We'll just have to take that chance."

"Chance!" Faranza appeared horrified. "You . . . you want to go out there?"

"It's the only way we're ever going to find out what's happening!" Deane said. "The question is, do we wait until those priests have left or do we take them by surprise while there's only the two of them? I don't want to leave the computer unguarded, it may be our only way to escape whatever force has brought us here."

Faranza rubbed his massive chin. "I could stay here while you follow them," he suggested, "or we could both surprise those two priests and question them about what's happened."

Deane searched his memory for a clue that would help him decide what to do, but all he could recall was the moment his finger had pressed the computer's key which had produced the hypnotic effects on the small screen.

Recall that moment with Steven Deane. Which key did he press? Was it the 1 key for NOVICE LEVEL? Or the 2 key for ADVANCED LEVEL? Or was it the 3 key for the EXPERT LEVEL of JAGUAR!

If you want to play JAGUAR at the NOVICE LEVEL, *turn to page 61*. If you want to play JAGUAR at either the ADVANCED or the EXPERT LEVEL, *turn to page 75*.

THE RETURN OF THE GODS

"We should take advantage of this opportunity to surprise that priest with the mask," Faranza suggested. "Even if he can't tell us what has happened, he seems to be an influential man and we might need his help if we are stuck here."

Deane realized that the sculptor's point was valid. They did not know what kind of dangers lay ahead of them, either inside or outside of the cavern. As an important man, the highpriest might be useful to them, even as a reluctant ally.

"O.K., let's take them," Deane agreed. He pushed his way past the Mayan's large body, wedging himself back into the best position for spying on the two priests.

"What are they doing?" asked the Mayan.

"The one called Cizin is cutting up the meat while his helper is watching," Deane whispered. "No, he's just marking the carcass. Now he's telling the fat one something about baskets. Oh, I see, he told the helper to butcher and pack the meat into two large baskets. Enul's cutting up the meat now."

Deane watched in silence a moment, then Faranza nudged him.

"What's happening now?"

"Cizin's walking through the cavern, smothering the torches."

"Then now's our chance!" Faranza whispered. "We could take the fat one easily and use him as a hostage, even if the other one runs."

Deane nodded his agreement and pushed on the concealed door. It opened noiselessly, permitting them both to step into the small space behind the red flickering wall.

Quietly they shut the portal, hiding the passage to the secret chamber, and crouched just inches from the pulsating curtain. It did not seem to be very thick, and they could see the priest's broad backside less than five yards away as he labored at his bloody task.

"NOW!" yelled Deane.

He and Faranza lurched forward at the luminescent barrier, shielding their faces in expectation of hitting something tangible, but they felt nothing at all. There was a bright flash of light as soon as their bodies penetrated the wall, followed by a thickening and darkening of the rose-colored mist around them. It swirled in billowing black-fringed clouds, hiding them and the cavern scene from each other.

It lasted only an instant before it began settling again, but by now the red wall was behind them. They had emerged on the opposite side, just behind the bloody altar stone and the priest.

Glancing curiously in back of himself, Deane saw that from this side, the "wall" appeared to be nothing more than a pulsating rectangle of red light and mist shimmering in front of a solid rock wall. There was no way to detect the entrance to the hidden chamber.

Faranza nudged Deane, who turned around abruptly. The fat cleric was staring at Deane and Faranza in terror, apparently rooted to the stone floor. Leaping forward, Faranza grabbed the junior priest, hoping to silence him before he recovered his senses. But as Faranza's heavy hand clutched the Indian's flabby biceps, the frightened man screamed.

"The real Shutec has come, Cizin! And his brother, Yopi, is killing me!"

The obsidian knife he had been using to divide the tapir's carcass flashed clumsily at the sculptor's chest.

Faranza dodged it easily. Catching the priest's wrist in his powerful grasp, Faranza forced him to drop the black blade onto the stone block.

Cizin, the highpriest, ran toward the altar, but then stopped in his tracks halfway down the cavern and dodged behind a large stalagmite to peer at the two strange creatures.

"Are you Shutec?" Cizin stammered. "Or do you come from the stars?"

"This is perfect!" Deane realized, wondering why this plan hadn't occurred to him all along. Copying the ancient vowels and consonants of the Olmecs as best he could, he said harshly, "Shutec and Yopi have come to punish those who use their names for deception!"

The highpriest's face paled, his eyes widened in fright.

"You must have mercy upon us, Lord Shutec," he cried. "We are your loyal servants in the Zoque priesthood at Talzok. When the Huasta invaded Zoque lands, many of your chosen people fell before the invaders' spears. We cried for your help, Shutec, and for yours, Yopi, but you left us to fight the Huasta alone. What could we do?"

"How many generations have passed since the Huasta enslaved the Zoque?" Deane demanded in his "godliest" voice, trying desperately to pinpoint a time.

"My lord, you must remember that the Huasta from the north first invaded the lowlands by the sea only in my father's youth," Cizin replied. "Your messengers from the stars appeared to him here, through the Wall of Mists, in that very year."

"What's he saying?" Faranza demanded with sudden impatience. The Mayan's English boomed in the cavern, producing an immediate change in Cizin's face.

"You are not gods!" he shouted. "You are 'Starmen!' "

"Watch out, he's going to run!" yelled Faranza.

63

Deane made a desperate leap for the highpriest, but Cizin was bounding across the open cavern, dodging around the torchlit cave formations with surprising agility for an old, emaciated man. He dashed into a lighted passage at the opposite end of the cavern and vanished, his muffled footfalls receding in the distance.

Deane returned to the altar where Faranza was guarding the fat priest. "Why did you scare him?" Deane demanded angrily.

As Deane drew near, Enul's eyes focused on the American's reddish-blonde hair and beard. With a groan, the superstitious cleric slumped unconscious into Faranza's arms, his great weight nearly causing the powerful Mayan to drop him.

"Damn! He's passed out!" Deane cursed, still perturbed by Faranza's oafishness. "Now we can't even ask him any questions!"

Studying the man's clothing, Deane tried to identify some of the ornaments and materials which had been used to make the crude garments. Beneath the lavish feathered headdress, the pudgy Indian wore his hair in long braids that were then tied together to form a black crest running along the center of his scalp.

Everything about the man's costume seemed authentic: untanned leather leggings, beadwork Deane had seen only in museums, beaten gold armlets worth thousands of dollars, and a breechclout which resembled a kilt dyed in multicolored patterns of orange and blue. It was all similar to early Mayan museum pieces and replicas, yet the styles were also different in major ways.

"Would you call these designs 'Mayan?' " Deane asked the sculptor, pointing to the loincloth. Faranza studied the lines from various angles and finally shook his head.

"I have never seen anything like those patterns before,

Steven," he said.

Deane was stunned. "Are you sure?" He had expected Faranza to recognize them as Olmec right away.

"Look at this mask, then," Deane told the sculptor, reaching for the heavy clay disk. "The ears are long and the eyes are slits, just as they are in most Olmec styles. This is either genuine, or it's the best reproduction of a ceremonial Olmec mask I've ever seen!"

Faranza took the mask and studied it closely. "If this is real Olmec, then any doubts you have about traveling into the past should be gone," said the Mayan sculptor. "This kind of sun-baked clay won't last more than a few years under the best of conditions. I can still see the fingerprints of the artist in several places. It looks real enough . . . Hey! He's moving!"

Deane saw the feathered headdress quiver and rise. Enul's eyes were glazed and his lips were trembling.

"Hold him, Luis! Don't let him escape!" Deane's sudden command thundered in the closed cavern, booming like the voice of a hundred gods or demons bellowing at the same time. As Faranza grabbed the frightened man around his thick waist, Enul started to shriek, twisting his body in panicked spasms to escape the Mayan's powerful grasp. But suddenly the man's struggles stopped. His tanned face contorted with pain, and he collapsed in Faranza's arms.

"Get him on the altar!" Deane ordered the Mayan. "I think he's had a heart attack!"

Sweeping the bloody baskets of meat to one side of the slab, Deane helped Faranza heave Enul's bulky body onto the low altar. Just as Deane reached out to try to resuscitate the cardiac victim, the sounds of running feet clamored from the torchlit entrance to the ritual chamber.

Cizin, the tall priest who had worn the clay mask, had

returned to the cavern bringing other men with him—the warriors Deane and Faranza had seen from the passage. All were armed with heavy obsidian spears and daggers. They poured into the chamber, surrounding the altar stone where the two strangers stood over the lifeless body of their befeathered priest.

Cizin pointed to Deane and shouted. "They are Starmen! Kill them before they can escape in the Wall of Mists!"

The closest warrior, a huge man, naked except for a leather apron and a cape of red and green feathers, motioned his companions forward with a sweeping gesture. Raising their black-tipped spears, they advanced toward the altar cautiously.

"Wait!" yelled Deane in desperation. "This man's had a heart attack. He may still be alive!"

Deane suddenly realized he had spoken in English in his panic, but apparently the booming sound was enough. The warriors stopped in their tracks and glanced nervously at each other. Ignoring them, Deane moved quickly, jerking the Indian's head backward by the hair and prying his lower jaw open. He reached into the man's mouth to clear the swollen tongue away from the throat and clamped his mouth over the other's bloodless lips.

A low murmur from the primitive warriors reverberated through the chamber. Deane worked at the alternating rhythms of breathing and chest pressure that make up the life-saving procedure of cardio pulmonary resuscitation.

Just as he was beginning to despair of saving the priest, Enul's heavy body began to convulse and heave. Deane grabbed the man's hair and pulled his head so that it hung over the edge of the altar stone while Enul gagged and vomited, clearing his windpipe in order to breathe again. Color returned to the priest's thick jowls and his eyes fluttered open. But when he saw Deane's wild-eyed, flushed face bent over him, he began to grow pale once more.

"Oh, no, not again!" exclaimed Deane. Reaching forward, he pushed the frightened man off the gory altar stone. The fat priest's feet struck the stone floor on the opposite side of the altar. Barely conscious, but still breathing, Enul tumbled into the arms of an astonished warrior. For a long, tense moment, the chamber was totally silent.

"What do you think they will do with us, Steven?" Faranza whispered softly. The Mayan's voice was cool. In situations involving the threat of physical danger, the giant sculptor was always confident.

"Your guess is as good as anybody's," Deane replied. "They came in here loaded for bear, but now they don't know what they want to do. Cizin told them we're 'Starmen,' whatever that means. It made them mad, but now they're confused. Of course, they don't understand CPR, so they probably think we've brought that guy back from the dead."

"Here comes the highpriest," Faranza mumbled.

Cizin was approaching the altar with his hands raised high above his head in a gesture of submission. Behind him, the warriors and the revived priest dropped to their knees with their foreheads pressed against the backs of their hands on the stone floor in front of them.

"Hail, Bringers of Life!" called the bald priest. "Hail, Shutec and Yopi! Command your servant, Cizin."

Deane and Faranza traded glances as they watched the gaunt holy man fall to his knees at the altar in front of the warriors. The Mayan leaned closer to whisper. "What did he say?"

"He thinks we're gods again. He called me 'Shutec,' the Olmec's supreme deity, and he thinks you're Yopi, Shutec's brother, the god of new life."

Faranza thought for a moment. "I don't trust the tall priest. He and his friend have been fooling these people, and now he knows we are taking their places. I don't think he really believes we're gods."

Deane nodded his head. "You may right about Cizin. He certainly gave in easily. And look how his eyes keep going to that wall of light behind us."

"I don't like that wall either, Steven." Faranza pouted. "It reminds me of the red light in your computer screen just before we came to this place."

"I don't like any this!" Deane snapped. "But there isn't a whole lot we can do!" He took a deep breath. "Look, I don't think the priests have any idea what's behind the wall. They seem to fear it too much to risk going through it, and the warriors are even more afraid of it. Maybe we can use that fear against them and take care of Cizin at the same time. Follow my lead. . . ."

Before the Mayan could answer, Deane grabbed the clay mask and leaped on top of the stone altar beside the two dripping baskets of fresh meat. Holding the huge mask high above his head, he shouted, "Behold the power of Shutec!"

As the warriors and the two priests stared at him in terror, Deane pointed at Cizin. "This mortal has dared to impersonate me with this mask!"

An angry muttering spread among the throng of fighters. The accused priest's eyes widened in fear as the warriors nearest him raised their obsidian-tipped spears.

"Wait, warriors of Talzok! Do not believe him!" Cizin cried. "He is an evil Starman like those who appeared to the Children of Chan and taught them to change themselves into beasts! He has come through the Wall of Mists to deceive and destroy us!"

Confused, the warriors looked from the highpriest to the

---

blonde stranger standing on top of the bloody altar. Deane saw now he had to act quickly. Turning, he threw the mask like a discus toward the rectangular patch of red light.

A brilliant white flash exploded on the surface of the energy wall when the heavy disk struck it. For the first time, Deane noticed a thick slab of white light rocket upward, moving so quickly it was almost invisible. It vanished instantly into a pinpoint of bright light high above the altar in the distant ceiling of the cave.

"See, men of Talzok," Deane proclaimed, remembering the name of their town from the highpriest's own words. "It is I, Shutec, who commands the Wall of Mists. You have been deceived by Cizin, who stands speechless before you. Bring him to the altar!"

The warriors closest to the highpriest grabbed his arms roughly and jerked him toward Deane. As they thrust Cizin forward, his head struck the edge of the carved block. Ignoring his cry of pain, the warriors left the dazed cleric kneeling at the feet of their greatest god, Shutec. One of the tallest fighters, a man with a hard, well-muscled body, stepped to the altar beside the stunned priest.

"Hear me, Lords Shutec and Yopi," called the powerful man. "I am Arras, your devoted servant. I know no prayers because I am a man of the spear and the dagger. Let my hand be the one to punish this stupid highpriest so that you do not bring your divine wrath upon our people. It was not we simple ones who dishonored you. Rather, it was Cizin. He is a false priest and must be slain."

The highpriest stood shakily, clutching the stained edge of the altar to stay on his feet. He raised his head to look at Deane, the blood from his gashed forehead mixing with the frightened tears on his taut cheeks.

"Lord Shutec, spare my life so that I may do penance for my deception. I did not mean to dishonor you, Skyfather. My only purpose was to maintain the agreement you yourself dictated to my grandfather and the Huasta chieftain years ago, to insure harmony between Zoque planters and Huastecan hunters."

Cizin's plea sounded earnest, but Deane saw a flicker of treachery in the man's cold eyes.

"Faranza's right," Deane thought. "This man could be either very dangerous or very valuable!"

"Arras and his warriors are young, Lord Shutec," Cizin continued. "They believe that the Zoque, your chosen people, are mere slaves. You have not visited us for many generations, and men like Arras must be reminded from time to time that you are real."

Arras's hand touched the magnificent polished jade hilt of a razor-edged black dagger he wore in the leather belt. The highpriest's patronizing attitude had apparently insulted the regal fighter, whose opinion of Zoque clerics was already dangerously low.

Deane looked at Cizin's bloodstained face with contempt and pity. He had heard the highpriest conspiring with his fat assistant during the ritual, and he knew how selfish their motives were. He wanted to show the shrewd cleric that he knew he was lying, yet without causing his execution. Both Arras and Cizin might be useful in helping him find answers to what was going on.

"Foolish priest!" Deane thundered. "Would you add to your crimes of deception by lying to a god? Have you not enjoyed the power and prestige of your people, not to mention their wealth, because of your impersonation of me?"

The warrior Arras's powerful left hand grabbed the gaunt highpriest's head and jerked it backward, exposing the terrified man's neck. Drawing his dagger, he raised it above the hapless priest's ashen face and looked expectantly at "Shutec." Deane gulped. He knew that the slightest signal would send the thin black blade plunging into Cizin's throat.

"Hold your dagger, brave Arras," Deane said hastily. "I have further need of this fool. He has learned his lesson. Your strength and your blade will serve me in other ways."

The fighter frowned in disappointment at the command. Relaxing his grip, he released the highpriest, who collapsed against the altar. Then, looking up at Deane, Arras fell to his knees before the blonde-haired man, who stood bathed in the red light of the pulsating wall.

"Lord Shutec," said Arras, "this deceitful priest told one truth among his lies. It has been too long since you have visited us. We have always spoken to you through false Zoque priests like Cizin. You have never talked directly to a man of Huasta before now, and we are truly honored. I beseech you, Lords, to return with us to Talzok in the Great Swamp. Live among us and teach us the ways and thoughts of gods!"

Deane jumped lightly to the floor of the cavern on the opposite side of the stone altar, next to Faranza. "Let's go somewhere we can talk. We've got a decision to make," he whispered quickly in Spanish. "They want us to go to their capital, a place called 'Talzok,' which may even be the birthplace of the entire Olmec civilization!"

The sculptor's eyes widened, but he said nothing. Turning back to the warriors, Deane raised his hands in the red-tinted air of the chamber to silence the mumbling group around the altar.

"Hear my words, Warriors of Talzok!" Deane called. "My brother, Yopi, and I must go to the place of gods beyond the Wall of Mists to fetch some sacred tools that will bring the people of Talzok great knowledge."

The warriors began to chatter even more loudly, pointing to the throbbing patch of red light. Arras seemed worried and called to Deane as he was turning toward the Wall.

"Lords! We ignorant soldiers fear that you will never return if you enter the Wall. We have sent many honored sacrifices by sending them to you through that Wall, but none have ever come back to us. Please do not desert your chosen people now that you have found them!"

Deane hesitated, wondering what Arras meant. The Wall was safe—he and Faranza had passed through it unharmed. Or was it?

"Your gods will not desert you as long as you believe in them, Arras," Deane replied. "Do not fear for Yopi and me. My brother and I have passed through the Wall many times through the centuries to visit mortals for purposes like these."

Then he turned to Faranza and patted his shoulder. "Come on, brother god, let's go to heaven." They stepped into the transparent patch of rose-tinted light. Just as when Deane threw the clay mask into the wall, a soundless flash of white light was the only sign that they had touched the red pulsing barrier. They passed through the mysterious wall without feeling anything, although they were surrounded briefly by the swirling, black-rimmed clouds.

Hurriedly, Deane and Faranza grasped the jagged edge of the hidden door and pulled it open, squeezing their bodies into the secret tunnel. Once inside the narrow corridor, Deane grabbed the metallic ring and pulled the heavy fake portal almost shut, leaving the same thin crack they had used before to spy on the gathering in the cavern.

"The clouds are thinning," Deane whispered. "I can already see their faces through the Wall of Mists."

The barrier became transparent again, revealing the astonished expressions of the barbarian fighters, who were staring in awestruck silence at the panel of light. Deane could imagine its appearance from the opposite side, having been surprised himself by its unusual visual effect. He knew they were seeing what they thought was a flat wall through a thick but transparent layer of red gel.

The only face that showed doubt was Cizin's, who gazed defiantly at the walls and ceiling all around the patch of ethereal mists. He appeared unready to admit to himself that Deane and Faranza had been real gods, perhaps because he knew how easy a role that was to play. Still, he seemed to fear the lighted barrier almost as much as Arras did, and was probably impressed by their use of it.

"What was all that conversation about?" Faranza asked. "I'm beginning to recognize some of the Zoque words, but I couldn't follow what you were saying."

Deane gave the sculptor a hasty summary of his confrontation with Cizin. "I think he's mystified by our use of the Wall. Neither the Zoque priests nor the Huasta warriors seem to know about this passage. They just use the Mists to send sacrificial victims 'to the gods.' Those victims never return."

"Then where are they?" asked Faranza, looking around in astonishment as if he expected to see the place filled with bodies. "If they didn't enter this tunnel and they never went back to their people, what happened to them?"

Deane felt a numbness in his head. Too many mysteries were piling on top of each other for him to handle at once: the latch of strange metal locked from inside the artificial tunnel, their teleportation three thousand years into the past, evidence of 'gods' and 'Starmen' who taught some people rituals and others to change into beasts. The only key he had was the computer program.

"Are you all right?" asked Faranza gruffly.

Deane shook his head. "No, and I won't be until we find out how we got here. The answer is inside that computer program. I'm sure of it! I need to study it, but at least one of us will have to go with them if we want to eat. I'm getting hungry, and there's no food in here!"

"It would be wiser if we stayed together in this strange place," Faranza suggested. "I still don't trust the one called Cizin. His fear of the warrior chieftain is the only thing making him accept you as 'Great Shutec.' If he ever gets the chance, he'll try to gain revenge for the humiliation you made him suffer. Human pride is a lot older than three thousand years, and you've wounded his!"

"We don't have to worry about Cizin as long as Arras believes in us," Deane muttered. "Still, you're right. We should keep an eye on him. But I'm don't want to leave the computer unguarded. There's bound to be someone else around here who knows about it—the same person or persons who moved us into the secret chamber. Until we discover who was responsible for that, and how they did it, we don't dare leave the equipment alone in this cave."

"So let's take it with us!" Faranza exclaimed, shrugging. "Your computer will mystify these primitives completely. There wouldn't be any doubts in any of their minds, including the highpriest's, that we're 'gods.' "

Steven Deane could take Luis Faranza's advice and leave the cave with the two priests and Arras's band of warriors, taking the computer with him. If this is your choice, *turn to page 115.* But if you think that Deane should stay behind, instead of going with Faranza and the others to "Talzok," *turn to page 133.*

THE WALL OF MISTS

"There's no reason why we should risk a confrontation with those spearmen," Deane told Faranza. "Let's give the warriors plenty of time to get wherever they're going. Then we can follow the priests and try to find both food and information."

Faranza grunted a noncommittal reply as he slumped against the tunnel wall. His classic Mayan face appeared stoic and hard in the periodic flashes of dull red light from the mysterious barrier.

Deane couldn't tell what he was thinking, but there wasn't time to worry about it. Turning back to look out the crack, he saw the highpriest, Cizin, standing at the altar, making lines on the huge carcass of the tapir with his obsidian dagger. After a few minutes, Cizin raised his bald head to stare at his fat underling.

"Get the baskets, Enul," ordered the highpriest.

Heading for a darkened corner of the cavern to the left of the altar, Enul reached into a low crevice and brought out two woven bags, each the size of a kitchen wastecan. By the time he had returned to the altar with the crude knapsacks, Cizin had finished his work.

"Butcher the animal while I extinguish the torches," he commanded the lesser priest. "I have marked the beast for your division of the meat. See that you follow my marks and load the baskets evenly."

Enul began cutting the carcass, fur and all, according to Cizin's scratches. He tossed the raw meat into the two baskets, alternating each piece to divide the weight evenly. Every scrap of meat and entrail was thrown into one or the other basket, leaving nothing for cave rats and other vermin. The blood from the hasty butchering job pooled and dripped from the flat top of the altar, adding yet another thickening layer to the dried and caked gore already there.

The cavern grew darker as Cizin doused torch after torch. Soon, Deane could see only one firebrand through the pulsating red curtain. The senior priest was holding it as he returned to the altar.

"Have you finished?" he asked Enul.

"Yes, my lord," he answered. "It is all packed except for the offering."

Cizin nodded and held out his hand. Enul extended his own hand, palm up, with something dark and glistening in it. Blood dripped and ran along the priest's fat arm as his superior took the gruesome object. The elder turned suddenly and faced the wall of glowing red mists. For a moment, it seemed to Deane that the priest was staring directly into his eyes, but then the cleric raised his face to the ceiling and shut his eyes to pray.

"Oh, Shutec, Firebringer, Altar-Guardian," he called in the Zoque-Huastec dialect, "receive the soul of this food which the barbarians have delivered to your faithful priests, and see that they continue to honor your temple with the ritual of meat and corn! We send this to you, through the Wall of Mists!"

At the conclusion of the short prayer, he hurled the dark object into the barrier of light. There was an instantaneous flash. The black-rimmed clouds of red mist surged upward again, rolling across the translucent wall until it seemed solid, yet alive. At the same instant, the "offering" landed on the floor of the niche just in front of Deane's feet, where he stood at the crack in the hidden door. It was the glistening heart of the tapir, its dark blood still oozing from the aorta onto the stone floor!

The swirling mists began to clear inside the opaque barrier a few seconds later. When the curious wall had become transparent enough to see into the cavern beyond, there was no sign of either priest.

"Come on!" Deane whispered to the Mayan. "They've gone!"

He pressed his body against the large slab, using his hand on the polished metal rung on the inner surface for leverage. Faranza's great bulk struck it, swinging the portal open so quickly that Deane tumbled forward into the niche behind the lighted barrier, his foot landing on the fresh heart which Cizin had "offered" to the god, Shutec. Slipping in the blood, Deane fell forward into the pulsating translucent curtain. There was a blinding flash, just as Faranza's voice yelled a startled curse behind him. For a moment, Deane was aware only of the red mists starting to darken around his face, then he was on the other side of the barrier, crashing into the bloody altar.

"Where are you, Steven?" Faranza called from the niche beyond the wall. Turning from the bloody stone, Deane stared back at the rectangular patch of red light.

"It's like a projector!" he murmured. The light seemed to be projected upon a solid wall of rock behind the altar. A faint pyramidal prism of light extended from the Wall of Mists to a steadily blinking pinpoint of bright light high in the ceiling of the cavern. Deane shielded his eyes with one hand, trying to determine the nature of the beam. It resembled the lamp of a distant motion picture projector, whose single bright spot became wider as it neared the screen.

"Can you hear me?" Faranza was bellowing.

"Be quiet!" Deane replied in a low voice. "Do you want those priests to call their friends with the spears? I'm just on the other side of the red curtain, and you'll be able to see me as soon as the fog clears."

The swirling mists were already settling. As the red rectangle of light became more transparent again, Deane could see the sculptor's huge figure standing only a few feet away. Behind him, the open panel appeared as a yawning hole delving darkly into the heart of the cavern. Faranza's body shimmered, looking as if he were on the other side of a doorway made of red Jell-O.

"Shut the secret panel," Deane called softly through the wall. The Mayan, relieved to see Deane, pushed against the specially carved boulder. It slid into place, completely concealing the tunnel which led to the hidden chamber with the computer and other equipment.

Then Faranza stepped quickly into the red wall. Once more, there was a sharp flash of light, but this time Deane watched as a flat plate of light shot upward at lightning speed toward the bright spot on the cavern ceiling among the countless stalactites. He tried to see if there was a change in the source of the projection when the light hit it, but it was lost in the brightness.

As before, a spectral prism of faint rose light remained as an afterimage. Faranza squinted at the bright blinking spotlight above them, then glanced at the pulsating square of red fog projected on the rocks behind them.

"It's a movie!" he exclaimed, forgetting to stifle his deep voice which now echoed throughout the chamber. "It's not radioactive, after all!"

"Quiet!" Deane hushed the giant. "It must be something like that. It may be designed just to help hide the entrance to that tunnel. You can't even see the niche in the wall behind the light, much less the opening. I'll trace the source of that light, but we don't have time to check it out now. Those two priests already have a ten-minute lead on us. Grab one of those torches!"

Faranza stepped quickly to the nearest torch, wedged tightly in a rock crevice, and jerked the firebrand loose.

Deane lit the gummy resin on its still-warm tip with his Bic lighter and the torch flared quickly, making the red glow of the projected wall fade slightly. Faranza waited for the flaming wood to stabilize, then he headed for the opposite side of the spacious cavern, while Deane followed.

They found an open passage, with the prints of many sandals and bare feet in the thin clay mud which had been tracked into the cavern from outside. Faranza thrust the torch into the tunnel, and Deane saw that it cut its way forward beyond the range of the flickering light.

"This must lead to the entry chamber," Faranza speculated. He started to continue but Deane hesitated at the entrance, staring behind at the bloody altar stone which glistened dramatically in the throbbing red light.

"Are you coming?" Faranza asked.

Deane glanced at the Mayan's excited face. The sculptor's off-handed remark about the red wall being a "movie" was bothering him. He was beginning to doubt his own first theory as well.

Faranza now seemed totally uninterested in the source of the lighted panel. But Deane was not at all satisfied about the nature of the red mists. He recalled that flat "bubble" of energy going toward the "projector," an impossible phenomenon for a normal projector. The more he thought about it, the more it didn't make any sense to him.

"I don't think so," he answered, not wanting to take the time to explain his reasoning to the impatient Mayan. "I'm still worried about leaving the computer here unguarded. We need to find food and scout the area, though. You go ahead and try to follow those priests while I do a little more checking around this cavern."

Faranza frowned and opened his mouth as if he were going to protest Deane's choice. Then he seemed to change his mind and—with a shrug—ducked into the tunnel. Deane waited for a few moments, listening to the Mayan's heavy footsteps recede into the distance. When the faint glow of his torch had vanished completely, Deane walked back toward the altar by the flashing red light of the projected barrier.

When he reached the roughly hewn boulder, he first examined its surface for clues to its manufacture. He saw immediately that it was not a limestone rock like the surrounding cavern walls. Instead, it was a huge block of basalt that had been transported here deliberately. The marks of crude chisels were obvious on the sides of the displaced monolith, reminding the scientist of similar marks on the unweathered bases of the huge stones at Stonehenge in England. There was nothing refined about this altar, like those excavated from Mayan and Olmec sites close to Monte Azul. It was much more massive and primitive than those intricately carved ceremonial stones.

"But this isn't any archeological find," Deane thought, his blood running cold. "This isn't very old at all, maybe only a few generations. And that tapir—an animal now extinct, but common three thousand years ago!"

Hurriedly Deane forced his reeling mind to concentrate on the problems at hand. Finding nothing more at the altar, he stepped cautiously around it and eased his way toward the strange patch of quivering and throbbing red light. It was as clear as tinted crystal, appearing to have the depth and mass of a gelatinous panel several inches thick. The outer surface was made of rays of rose-tinted light which streaked either from or to a brilliant apex high above the altar.

Picking up a discarded cornstalk on the cavern floor, Deane probed the beam with one end of it. He expected to see a flash of light like before, but it did not happen. In fact, nothing happened. There was not the slightest disruption of the projected panel's surface, not even a shadow.

"So much for the movie projector theory," Deane thought. "If that thing was a projection, the cornstalk should have cast a shadow on it!"

More puzzled than ever, he slowly extended the stalk until its end barely prodded the strange surface of the ethereal red gel. Predictably, a flare of white light exploded soundlessly at the tip of the cornstalk. This time, he watched carefully as the light contracted into a rectangular "bubble" and shot upward at lightning speed. It ascended so quickly that he lost it almost immediately in the bright but distant spotlight above the stone altar.

STOP!

If Steven Deane is playing JAGUAR! at the ADVANCED LEVEL, *turn to page 82*. But, if Deane selected the EXPERT LEVEL in the computer program, *turn to page 94*.

THE WEREJAGUAR

Deane was even more confused. Logically, the thick "curtain" could not be a projection; if it were anything like that, there had to be a projector! The flow of the energy seemed to be away from the rectangular barrier rather than toward it. The pinpoint of light was apparently the source of unknown signals transmitted upward to some kind of receiver located at the apex of the pyramidal beam of rose-tinted light.

Deane noticed that the Wall of Mists was positioned so that anyone exiting from the hidden chamber would have to pass through it. At first, he thought it might be a barrier, an energy shield of some kind, designed to keep people in the chamber prisoners. Now, Deane was beginning to believe it was simply a monitoring device, keeping track of anyone coming or going through the red wall.

"Whoever engineered the alteration of that computer program must have planned this entire situation," he guessed, "and that's who's up there on the other end of the beam. It's nothing more than a sophisticated alarm system!"

Gazing upward, he tried to detect signs of movement, but there was only the unwavering rhythm of the light pulses.

"I've got to get outside to find it," he thought. "There must be a level of the cave higher than this one, and that's where the receiver of the signals is located. Once I find it, I'll know who or what is monitoring that wall."

Running to the right side of the cavern, Deane jerked another torch from its wedged position along the wall. He paused long enough to light it with the Bic, then trotted back to the entrance to the outer tunnel. With a final glance at the dramatic view of the strobe-lit altar, he ducked into the passage which Faranza had taken several minutes earlier.

The narrow corridor continued straight ahead for nearly fifty feet. The thin layer of wet clay on the stone floor grew thicker and more slippery with each step. At the end of the straight stretch, the tunnel swerved to the right, making an almost ninety-degree turn, then swung back again to the left. In the torchlight, he could see a dark, narrow fissure at the dead end of the passage.

The entry corridor twisted up a slight incline before leveling off at the narrow exit. Water had seeped into the cave at places, making the floor even more slippery. Deane had nearly reached the exit fissure when his worn and muddy sandals completely lost their traction. His feet slipped out' from underneath him.

Deane thrashed at the tunnel walls, trying to stop himself from falling. But he succeeded only in dunking the torch into a pool of stagnant water as he fell forward onto his stomach. He lay there a moment, recovering his breath and cursing the loss of his light. But as his eyes recovered from the sudden change, he realized that the darkness was not as thick as it had been.

"I must be near the mouth of the cave," Deane realized as he saw gray light coming from the slit at the end of the passage.

Grabbing the torch, he tried to light it, but it was so soaked that even its resinous tip would not ignite. Finally, he quit trying and tossed it away. Deane struggled to his feet. Finding better footing, he stumbled up the incline and through the fissure into an entry chamber as large as a big living room The floor was still slippery but level enough to stand and rest.

Just ahead, he could see either dawn or dusk light filtering through the branches of trees outside the rounded mouth of the cavern. He had taken only two steps toward the entrance when a human figure suddenly appeared in the opening and stood staring at him. The figure was robed, but showed no signs of either fear or reverence, as the warriors and priests had displayed inside the altar chamber.

"Is it the great god Shutec who confronts me, or Cizin, the monkey of a priest who deceives the people of Talzok for his own benefits?" the figure called.

It was the voice of a woman, speaking the ancient Zoque-Huastec patois.

Deane thought quickly. The woman had given him an idea.

"It is I, Shutec. And I have chastized Cizin for his treachery," replied Deane hastily. "He is an impure priest, just as you say, and will no longer be allowed to steal meat in my name!"

Deane hoped he had not overplayed the role. The woman in the cavern entrance took two or three steps forward until she was far enough inside the mouth to stand aside and let dim sunlight strike the American's reddish-golden hair and beard. Deane could see her lithe female figure outlined through the thin fabric of her long white gown by the gray light behind her, but could not see her face as she could his.

"YOU!" she cried suddenly in a coarse whisper. "Why have you followed me through the Wall of Mists? Do you know what you've done?"

The woman's unexpected words shocked Deane so completely that he forgot his role as Shutec. Thrusting his lighter toward her face, he thumbed the wheel. She shrieked in astonishment and threw her hands in front of her in a protective reflex. But in the instant before she had shielded herself, the bright orange flame revealed to Deane the face of a breathtakingly beautiful woman, surrounded by cascades of dark shimmering hair.

She could not be more than twenty or twenty-five years old, from the look of her youthful and trim body. Her low-cut gown was made of a loosely woven white cloth and a highly polished jade pendant hung between her youthful breasts. Deane stared at the jewel in amazement. The glassy jewel hanging from her neck was carved in the design of the half-human, half-feline werejaguar!

"How does she know me? I've never seen her before," Deane thought in confusion. Then he realized suddenly that since she knew he had crossed the Wall, she must also know about the chamber behind it!

"Who are you?" he demanded. "What do you know about the Wall of Mists? How do you know me?"

Her dark eyes narrowed as the strange woman studied Deane's anxious expression. Then, seeing his eyes on her jaguar medallion, she suddenly grabbed it between her palms as if she wanted to hide it.

"Talk to me!" Deane urged excitedly. "What is this place? Why are you trying to hide that necklace?"

The woman slowly parted her hands and glanced at the pendant, its surface flashing in the light of the Bic. A look of panic suddenly contorted her beautiful features. Stifling a cry that seemed to be one of dismay rather than alarm, she whirled and dashed outside the cave.

"WAIT! STOP!" Deane yelled, but the woman had vanished. He ran after her.

The entrance to the cave was situated on a ledge of a mountainside dotted with boulders and slabs of grey limestone. In front of the cave entrance, the slope was so steep that only scrub trees and hardy shrubs could hang on to the rocky soil. A precarious path skirted the ledge and continued along the face of the mountain in both directions.

The prints of countless naked toes and feet were easy to see in the afternoon sun. It was obvious that the beautiful woman had run either right or left, but Deane did not know which way. The path was relatively straight and clear for nearly thirty yards in both directions. Deane stared around.

There were ample boulders and bushes in both directions to hide someone, especially in the failing light. Tossing a mental coin, he turned to the left and had taken less than half a dozen steps when a blur of white darted across the path just ahead. It was the woman, climbing the steep slope beside the cave.

As Deane ran up the mountainside after her, she glanced over her shoulder at him and he saw her face clearly for the first time. Its wild, frightened-animal look added to the Indian woman's natural beauty. Her long black hair glistened in the last rays of sunset, casting a reddish aura around her head.

She gathered her long white robe with her hands, pulling it higher to free her legs. Then she darted nimbly to the side, heading for the next ledge. The woman moved with the agility of a mountain goat and the bounding strides of a deer fleeing for its life. The muscles of her slender legs rippled smoothly beneath the tanned skin of her calves and thighs.

"Stop! I'm not going to hurt you!" Deane shouted as the terrified woman scrambled up the steep slope. He climbed after her. Though out of condition, he was still a fast runner. Yet he was unable to catch this lithe Indian woman as she traversed the rugged terrain.

Every few moments, he could see her glance over her shoulder at her pursuer. Deane's heart was pumping strongly as his breathing slipped into the regular, measured rhythms of a marathon runner. The race had become a serious one for him, perhaps because of the taunting half-smile he now saw on the woman's face each time she glanced at him behind her.

"She's playing with me!" he realized suddenly. "She knows that I can't catch her!"

The slope was getting gentler. They were nearing the top of a ridge where a high plateau forest extended for as far as Deane could see in all directions, except the one from which he had come. The woods around them had grown completely still except for the steady sounds of the two pairs of feet thrashing the dry leaves and grass on the crest of the ridge. The forest seemed to grow thicker in the direction they were running. Deane felt his lungs get their second wind and decided to make his best bid to catch her before she reached the heavier cover. He began to concentrate on his stride and cadence, moving his legs faster.

His muscles responded to his forgotten athletic training, as if they had memories of their own, pumping mechanically at a steadily higher rate. Deane's concentration upon his competitor was total. The gap between the two runners began to close. The woman's smile faded as soon as she realized what was happening. In one rapid movement, she stripped off her bulky robe and cast it aside on the forest floor. Deane could see her tanned nude figure dodging through the deepening shadows, running faster now without the cumbersome garment bunched around her hips.

Deane tried to force his legs to move more quickly by focusing all of his willpower on them. Sweat was pouring into his eyes, blurring his vision so that he could barely see the slender body darting through the thickening trees. But he was growing tired and began to stumble, losing his footing on the cluttered forest floor. He was watching the ground, trying to avoid the larger fallen branches and logs when he saw the rope stretched across his path only an instant before it cut into his chest. Deane fell to the ground with crushing force. The back of his head slammed against the hard earth, and everything went black.

Throbbing pain merged in Deane's head with a rhythmic chant. Behind his shut eyelids, he had a dim sensation of flares and a flickering light from an open fire. As his awareness sharpened, the heat warned him, telling him that the fire was close, perhaps less than a dozen yards away from where he lay on the hard clay ground.

Before opening his eyes, he gently tried to separate his hands, only to discover that they had been trussed behind his back! A bolt of panic surged in his brain when he tensed his leg muscles. His ankles were tied just as tightly as his wrists!

Forcing his mind to control the fear that was spreading into every muscle and nerve cell of his body, Deane made himself concentrate on every detail he could sense with his eyes closed. He was lying on his left side, bound securely and facing a fire several yards away. From the sound of the chanting voices, he was surrounded by a number of males. Listening to their singing, he tried to distinguish the words.

It came back to him in a rush of confused memories. They were using the same ancient Olmec dialect Aruca and Trago spoke—the same one spoken by the warriors and priests of Talzok as well as by the woman he had been chasing. He opened an eyelid slightly to see his captors, who were chanting in the prehistoric language the Olmec used three thousand years ago!

With his cheek pressed against the ground, Deane could see only feet and hands shuffling first toward, then away from him in the firelight. The men seemed to be growling and making ritual charges at him on all fours, in imitation of some wild animal!

The feet and hands were getting closer. Deane felt cold sweat burst onto his forehead when he saw golden talons strapped to the fingers and toes! They were sharpened replicas of jaguar claws, tied to the dancers' hands and feet by thin strips of leather. As they moved closer to him with each surge of chanting, Deane's eyes widened in panic and desperation.

"GET BACK!" he screamed.

With a sudden burst of energy, Deane staggered to his hobbled feet and faced the startled throng. The dancers ceased chanting abruptly and stood staring glassy-eyed at the bearded stranger. Deane scanned the scene around the campfire. Most of the chanters were men, naked except for leather breechclouts and ragged, dirty jaguar pelts draped across their brown shoulders. Their dark eyes were glazed, either with fear or perhaps by some unknown narcotic.

Near the fringe of the dancers' circle, two women stood beside a raised stone slab, probably an altar. Even from this distance, Deane could see the gruesome brownish stains which almost covered the flat surface. One of the women was the same one he had chased from the temple cave. She wore her long white robe again, and had added a magnificent jaguar pelt with head and claws still attached. The head was tied onto her own skull, while the forepaws were fashioned into taloned mittens. Her companion was a withered old woman dressed in the same fashion.

"Untie me!" Deane commanded in a loud voice, using the Olmec dialect.

The astonished dancers seemed even more confused when he spoke. Many of them frowned and some took a few uncertain steps backwards. Several of the men mumbled to each other but made no attempt to follow their captive's orders.

"They will not hear your words, golden-skinned man."

The old woman was striding toward him, pushing her way through the dazed male dancers. The woman he had chased followed at her heels and appeared to be either shy or frightened as the two approached their captive. Stepping closer to Deane, the elder pointed to her younger companion.

"My priest-sister, Aruca, fears that you have brought the wrath of Chan, the Jaguar God, upon us by spying on her at the altar," she said softly, as if that would explain everything that had happened.

"Spying on her?" Deane cried. "I've never even seen her before! The only 'Aruca' I know is . . ."

Deane gasped.

"My God!" he thought. " 'Aruca . . . 'priest-sister'! Could this be the 'Aruca' I saw near Monte Azul—the old woman I watched change into a jaguar?"

He forced himself to imagine the beautiful young girl as the same arthritic old woman whose spell he had recorded three days ago. "Or is that three thousand years from now?" he added, on the verge of hysteria. Deane began to feel as if he were trapped in a nightmare. He was having trouble thinking coherently, yet he knew his life depended on what he did next.

He decided his best course was to keep up the charade he had already started.

"Tell your 'priest-sister' that Chan, the Jaguar God, sent me to watch over her," he said quickly. "I was there to . . . to protect her."

"How do we know that you were not sent by that fiend Trago instead?" the young woman challenged.

"Trago!" Deane's mind reeled. "Miguel Trago? What could that old hermit have to do with this?" he asked himself. Then he began to reflect on things more calmly. Everything that had happened to him over the past two days appeared to be connected—Aruca, Trago, these people, the Huastecan warriors, the Zoque priests, the computer, the wall of red mists! But how did the pieces of this puzzle fit together?

"If . . . uh . . . Trago did send me, he would know what is happening to me. He would try to help me, wouldn't he?" Deane suggested, hoping to find out more about Trago.

The young woman nodded gravely. "Trago's wrath toward the Children of Chan cannot be measured, and what you have said is true. Trago's vision is without limits. If he knew of your capture, he would have already attempted to rescue you. You cannot be Trago's servant, nor can you be a mere human. Only the most foolish of mortals would enter the Wall of Mists unprotected by Chan, and none could escape Trago's wrath."

"The Wall of Mists again!" thought Deane. "They must be some kind of gate into time, and involved somehow with what happened to Faranza and me!"

"You have guessed the truth, Priest-Sister of Chan," Deane said in grave tones. "But even Trago does not dare confront the power of Shutec," he added with a direct reference to the powerful Olmec fire deity whom the priest in the cave had impersonated.

A flicker of emotion flashed in the young woman's black eyes. She paused for a moment as if she were deciding whether or not to believe him. Finally she pulled an obsidian dagger from a pocket in the jaguar pelt and slashed at Deane's arms. The razor edge had scarcely touched the leather thong binding Deane's wrists when the heavy fiber snapped apart.

"Return to the temple, servant of Shutec," said the old

priestess to Deane. "Tell the Skyfather that his grandchildren, the sons and daughters of Chan, honor his name and seek only to protect ourselves from the demonic powers of Trago. Free the Starman's feet, too, Priest-Sister."

"Starman!" Deane thought wearily. "Now I'm a Starman, whoever that is!"

Rubbing his wrists to restore their circulation, Deane watched the younger priestess drop to her knees and cut the thong which hobbled his ankles. Aruca's nearness excited and tantalized him. As she bent to free him, the loose gown fell away from her firm breasts. Her thick hair draped across his thighs for only an instant, but it had the impact of a lover's caress.

"Aruca pleases the 'golden man,' " the old woman said softly.

Deane looked away from the younger priestess's hair and breasts, feeling an embarrassed blush spread from his neck to his cheeks. Aruca raised her head, her lovely features frowning slightly when she finally understood what her elder companion had meant. She stared at Deane with an irritated expression in her eyes, but relaxed when she saw his flushed complexion. He might be a messenger from Shutec, or a "Starman," but he was still just a man and Aruca apparently recognized his vulnerability to her wild beauty.

"Ask the servant of the Fiery One for Shutec's blessing, Aruca," ordered the old priestess.

The young woman bowed to her superior and reached for the American's hand. Then she pulled the outstretched palm closer until its heel touched her forehead. Deane realized suddenly that she was demonstrating the proper form of a blessing. He then reached toward her elder companion and pressed his hand against her scalp in the same way.

Both priestesses dropped to their knees. All around

them, the crowd of male dancers muttered nervously among themselves at the sight of this display of subservience by their powerful priestesses to this man, who had been a captive only moments before. Sensing the perfect moment to leave, Deane turned away from the women with both arms outstretched high above his head.

"Let the blessings of Shutec be upon all the servants of Chan!" he intoned solemnly, remembering the performance of the masked priest inside the cave. The cultists' eyes widened in a mixture of religious fear and awe as they dropped instantly, prostrating themselves face down on the hard clay of the dance ground.

Stepping carefully around the men, Deane worked his way toward the fringe of the clearing. At the edge of the light from the campfire, where the trees and undergrowth were thicker, he paused and glanced back to make sure the cultists were not following. The men were still lying face-down, too frightened to move, but both women were watching him intently. Their expressions of religious awe were gone, replaced by those of doubt and curiosity.

Deane turned and dodged into the deeper shadows of the forest, trying to decide what to do as he put a cautious distance between himself and the camp of the jaguar cultists.

He could return to the clearing and remain among the Children of Chan to learn more about their cult—and about the beautiful Aruca. If this is Deane's decision, *turn to page 152.* Or Deane could go back to the cave and wait for Faranza to return with food and his report. If this is Deane's decision, *turn to page 163.*

MIGUEL TRAGO

Deane studied the surface of the patch as the turbulent clouds of red mist settled, leaving behind the appearance of quivering gelatin. Once again, the twinkling dot of brilliant light was connected to the barrier by a faintly blinking, rose-colored ray.

Deane had an idea. This might be the source of unknown signals which were transmitted upward to some kind of receiver located at the apex of the pyramidal beam.

He noticed that the Wall of Mists was positioned so that anyone leaving the hidden chamber would have to pass through it. At first, he thought it might be a barrier, an energy shield of some kind, designed to keep those inside the chamber prisoner. Now, Deane was beginning to believe it was simply a monitoring device.

"Whoever engineered the alteration of that computer program must have planned this entire situation," he guessed, "and that's who's up there on the other end of the beam. It's a sophisticated alarm system!"

Deane began to search the cavern walls for a passage of some kind that would lead to the ceiling. He was so intent upon his task that he failed to notice the instantaneous flare of light from the transparent barrier by the altar.

"You will not discover the path to Monte Azul among those shadows, Senor Deane!"

The sudden sound of a man's strong voice in heavily accented Spanish shocked Deane so badly that his heart seemed to leap into his throat. Jerking his head toward the voice, which was coming from the direction of the altar, he saw a thin figure silhouetted against the red pulsations of the opaque wall behind the hewn boulder.

Someone had just stepped through the barrier! The face

was shrouded in shadows so that Deane could see not more of its features than a hawkish outline of gaunt cheekbones, a protruding chin, and a high-bridged nose. It appeared to be a man wearing loose white campesino garments and a wide-rimmed woven hat.

But the stranger's voice sounded familiar! Deane knew that he had heard it before.

"I detect a puzzled reaction," the man said. "Is it possible that you do not understand me? Is my Spanish not correct?"

"Your Spanish is perfect," Deane answered in the same language. "Pardon me for not responding to you. I was only trying to place your accent and speech. I'm a linguist and I've heard a lot of Mexican Spanish dialects, but yours is a new one."

The man was using a stiff, formal version of Spanish common only among educated Mexicans of the late nineteenth century. Deane remembered reading the texts of speeches by prominent Mexican statesmen from that period and recalled the use of certain archaic verb tenses that this man was also using.

"Ah, then you must have an excellent ear for sounds of speech. You have recognized my outdated expressions. I have always thought it such a tragedy that linguistic change often takes the direction of corruption. I merely refuse to allow my Spanish to be modernized, Senor Deane."

"No, there's something else. I've met you before, haven't I? Your face is in shadows but your voice is distinctive. You appear to know me but I can't recognize you."

"Excellent! Your ear is even better than I thought! Perhaps this will refresh your memory."

The tall silhouette suddenly hunched forward beside the bloody altar stone, assuming the posture of a withered

---

peasant. Deane recognized the man instantly, even before he spoke in the rural Zoque dialect.

"My throat is dry, patron. Perhaps another glass of tequila?"

It was Miguel Trago! Deane took several steps closer to the old man he had interviewed in the cantina at Monte Azul. As he approached the altar, Trago raised his head and turned it slightly toward the lighted wall behind him. The red glare shone in his eyes and cast its rosy pulsations over the craggy face which now bore a sardonic smile.

"Who are you?" Deane demanded. "You're no illiterate hermit! What do you know about this place?"

"Be silent for a moment," Trago replied in a cool unhurried voice that compelled Deane to comply with the soft command. "First, I wish to apologize for leaving you so abruptly at Monte Azul. You may imagine how astonished I was that you had chanced upon such a secret act of compulsion as my sister's."

"Your sister? Aruca? The woman who changed into a jaguar?"

"There are some inaccuracies in the way you refer to that episode, but for the moment, yes—we speak of the same Aruca. My sister has a . . . a malady which has plagued her for a considerable time. I have tried to help her control the course of the disease, and your recording of her intimate prayers revealed a truth which I was unwilling to hear—namely, that I had failed. I fled your company, not in rage, but in bitter disappointment. My sister's secret is too dangerous to share with anyone in your world. I needed solitude to consider my best reaction to your access to that knowledge."

"*Your* world," thought Deane. "Why *your* world? Why not *our* world?"

But there was another, more important question on his

mind. "How did you hypnotize my assistant and me?" Deane blurted. "How did you manage to bring us here, into the past? Because we *are* in the past, aren't we?"

Trago straightened his tall figure. "I did not bring you anywhere, Senor Deane. I followed you. And I know nothing of hypnosis, which is a minor conjurer's trick."

"Then who did bring us here?" Deane demanded. "We certainly didn't manage to travel three thousand years into the past on our own!"

Trago smiled. "Ah, you've deduced the approximate displacement. Excellent!"

"To hell with the 'displacement,' Trago! Talk! Who's behind this and why? What are you doing here?"

The hermit's smile faded to a serious expression. "Don't you see? No one 'brought' you here. I fear that the key to your dilemma lies in the cyphering machine you call a 'computer.' It is a more powerful device than you may realize, one which can produce unpredictable effects. But you know more about such an apparatus than I."

Deane stared suspiciously at the mysterious man who spoke Zoque as well as nineteenth century Spanish. The bony features were highlighted against the blinking backdrop of lighted red gel, reminding Deane strongly of someone playing a sinister sorcerer in a fantasy movie. He didn't trust Trago, but the man obviously held answers to his questions.

"Well, since you followed us, you must know where we are," said Deane. "My field assistant has gone to scout our exact location, but perhaps you might have saved him the effort. Maybe you could also show us how to return to our own time?"

"I do indeed know your location, both in time and in space, Senor Deane. Unfortunately, it is impossible for me to give you that information in words you will understand.

I will only say that your Senor Faranza's task is futile. He is searching in the wrong direction. The path back to your village and your time lies there, through the 'Wall of Mists,' as it is known here."

Trago pointed toward the pulsating patch of light behind the altar. Then he extended a bony hand to the linguist.

"Let me show you the way home. I cannot tell you where you are, nor can I tell you how to return, but I can take you back."

The man's skeletal-looking hand repelled Deane almost instantly. He pulled away reflexively, causing Trago to drop his arm.

"If you do not trust me," he observed in a tired voice, "how can I help you?"

"Perhaps I just don't understand you," corrected Deane. "I need to understand someone before I trust him. And even if I did trust you, I wouldn't leave Faranza and my—"

Deane caught himself, not wanting to mention the computer. It and the diskette might still be the only way back to Kaktunque and he wanted to keep it hidden.

"You were going to say 'computer,' I believe," Trago finished for him. "Do not be alarmed. I knew the moment you arrived here that the apparatus was with you. In fact, as I have suggested, the machine is probably responsible for your, umm, displacement, shall we say?"

"How can a machine be responsible for this 'displacement?' It takes a human to program a computer!"

Trago waved his hand. "That is truly a question for someone with more technical knowledge of these things than I have. However, as I told you a while ago, these cyphering machines are much more powerful than you might realize. But, there is not enough time for philosophical discussion just now. You must accompany me through the Mists. I fear that your assistant and your machine must remain here. He is lost, at least for the moment, and the computer will not. . . umm. . . fit the dimensions of the passage we must take."

"What dimensions?" demanded Dean. "If it got here that way, I should be able to take it back the same way."

"You have heard my words incorrectly, scholar. I did not say that you arrived by way of the Wall; I merely said that was the only way I knew for you to return."

"I don't understand what you're saying," shouted Deane in frustration. He forced himself to calm down. "All right, let's skip the computer for a moment." Pointing to the quivering red wall behind Trago, he asked, "What is that stuff behind the altar? What makes it glow with those rhythmic beats? And why is it connected to that light in the ceiling?"

The man's mouth twisted with a trace of a smile. "Those are three separate questions, one easy to answer and the other two impossible to know. First, let me dismiss those which I cannot answer. The 'stuff,' as you call it, has no substance to analyze. It is what it appears to be—a formless, weightless mist composed of a type of energy unknown to your material sciences. There are only very few places in the entire world where the Wall has appeared, and this is one of them. As for the glow, I cannot even begin to understand such a thing. Through the ages, humans have appealed to their belief in higher beings to 'explain' the existence of the Wall itself, seldom daring to penetrate the mystery further and examine its interior."

"I don't have the slightest idea what you're talking about," declared Deane. "That barrier must have sub-stance. Look at it quivering like a dish of Jell-O!"

"Jell-O? I do not understand that word."

"It's a dessert made of colored, sweetened gelatin,"

Deane explained, having to search his memory for the Spanish word 'jaletina'.

"A splendid visual analogy!" Trago exclaimed. "Yes, it would seem gelatinous to you, I suppose. But I assure you that its tactile properties are nonexistent to the human sensory system. The Wall of Mists has always existed, as have other rare gates such as this one."

Suddenly Trago's explanation began to form itself into a bizarre pattern inside Deane's mind.

"Are you saying that this Wall of Mists is some kind of gate to another time?" he demanded.

"It is more complicated than that, scholar. The forces within the Wall can be controlled with your will, but it requires great concentration. I have traveled the mists many times, and I understand their flow. Take my hand and let my thoughts guide you homeward. But hurry. I must seek my sister before she is beyond my powers to . . . help."

Deane might have interpreted Trago's hesitation with the word "help" as mere forgetfulness if he had not seen the hermit's eyes flash when he uttered it.

Remembering ancient "cures" for werewolves, Deane shuddered. Did Trago have that sort of cure in mind for his sister's "disease?" Thoughts of silver bullets and stakes through hearts flew through Deane's mind. Then he shook his head. He was letting this strange situation get to him!

"Are you coming? We must hurry!" Trago insisted, and Deane could detect a hint of anger. "Or are you going to stay here?"

Deane hesitated. He hated leaving Faranza and the computer, but surely there must be ways of returning! After all, Trago apparently traveled through this "gate" frequently. And this might just be the clue he needed to explain what was going on! Making his decision, Deane stepped forward.

Trago's slender brown fingers grasped the linguist's palm with a firm, leathery grip and pulled the younger man toward the pulsating wall with such surprising ease that Deane felt a twinge of alarm at the old man's great strength.

"Think only of my hand," Trago commanded. "You must tell your mind that you want only for my hand to guide you through the Wall of Mists."

Trago's compelling voice cut into Deane's thoughts like a steel saber into unarmored flesh. He focused entirely on the strong grip of the hermit's powerful fingers, just as the old man had commanded. Though Deane could not remember walking, he and Trago must have stepped together into the glowing red barrier. There was an instant flash, just as before, but this time it did not end with his standing in the niche before the secret door. Instead, they seemed to hover in a weightless state, surrounded by swirls and eddies of the reddish mist which had neither form nor substance. The unyielding grip of Trago's hand was the sole material sensation Deane felt.

"Where are . . ."

"The hand! Think only of the hand!"

The hermit's harsh reminder stifled Deane's question instantly, but not before he witnessed the slightest parting of the seething red-black opaque substance surrounding them. In that brief moment, Deane thought he had also seen and heard the flash of steel and the cries of wounded animals. The glimpse had been too brief for him to identify the flashing scene, but it remained in his subliminal brain as they continued their unusual journey into the Wall of Mists.

In the same remote corner of his mind, Deane was conscious of Trago's thoughts dominating his own. It was a sweeping sensation which left him feeling as passive and powerless as a leaf in a stream. Yet it was also strangely pleasant to surrender mindlessly to a force more potent than any he had ever experienced, including gravity. It was even mildly disappointing when he felt the pressure on his hand decrease and the eerie sensation of motion without movement began to fade.

"Look at your feet," Trago commanded. "Put them on the ground next to mine."

Deane stared dazedly at the tops of his light huarache sandals, which had long since replaced the hot, heavy field boots he had brought to Yucatan from Boston. He moved them sluggishly at first, as if he had lost control of his leg muscles. Finally he was able to command them to do his will, though it required a deliberate effort to shift them to the side of Trago's even dustier sandals. He was looking at his feet, it seemed, through the wrong end of a telescope so that they appeared to be smaller than usual and farther away. Both pairs of huaraches were floating in the red mist when he started moving toward the hermit's side, but as Trago's words echoed in his brain, a floor of stone materialized beneath them.

He stumbled forward, out of the Wall of Mists, behind Trago's slender figure. They were still in the cavern, but it was not the same dismal place he had left only moments before. The ritual chamber was now ablaze with so many cloth-bound torches that their bright light stifled the rosy pulses of energy from the Wall.

The massive altar was still there in front of the dimensional gate, but it had been embellished by some unknown artists with complicated designs and detailed human figures, wondrously carved in the hard black basalt. In the body of the brightly lit cavern, Deane could see that the scores of stalagmites had been sculpted into stelae, those pillars of stone carved into the shapes of humans by the Maya, Aztec, and Olmec people to record their histories.

"This can't be the same cavern!" Deane thought. "It would have been impossible to carve all of these things in the brief time we spent inside the Wall, even with an army of professional sculptors!" But then he noticed the familiar layout of the cavern, particularly the unchanged stalactites hanging from the ceiling. There could be no doubt in his mind. This was the same cave he and Faranza had first seen after they awoke in the secret chamber with the computer.

"Can you decipher these designs, scholar?" Trago asked, noticing Deane's interest.

The linguist crouched beside the large altar and studied the workmanship, trying to compare it to the images stored in his memory of similar offering stones from other parts of Mexico. He knew immediately that it was not Aztec, but was unsure about possible Mayan influences. The faces seemed more "oriental" than Indian, one of the major features which distinguished Olmec sculpture.

Deane left the altar and began studying the stelae closest to it. He knelt on the rocky ground, studying the pictographs which wound their way around the carved pillars of limestone. Many of the designs were disturbingly familiar, yet they seemed out of place. They were not classic Mayan stelae at all, yet he was absolutely sure that he had seen something like them before.

The scientist moved around the chamber, occasionally dropping to his knees to examine a carving more closely in the bright torchlight. He soon noticed that the stelae nearest the altar was more worn—older, perhaps—than those on the outer perimeter of the cavern. He also discovered an important similarity among some of the carved faces on the innermost stelae. They had all been rendered as a broad-faced race with thick lips, wide noses and wearing round helmets which Deane suddenly realized were very similar to those worn by the warriors he and Faranza had seen earlier. They were almost identical to the massive stone heads which had become accepted as a key trait of the Olmec!

"Well?" Trago queried. "Have you reached a conclusion about these sculptures, Senor Deane?"

"I think they're Olmec," he said, after hesitating several seconds, "and if I'm right, this is the largest Olmec site ever discovered, perhaps even the original center of Olmec influence in Mexico!"

Trago smiled slightly. "Come with me to my quarters. I have something to show you which may alter your opinion of these things." The old man started walking toward the rear of the cavern, but Deane was reluctant to leave his valuable find.

"Come, come!" Trago urged. "You will be able to study these carvings whenever you like. There are other questions, both to ask and to be answered."

He led Deane to a well-lighted tunnel at the edge of the chamber with the stelae. Deane suddenly recognized it as the same passage which Faranza and the others had taken to reach the entrance of the cave. After several hundred feet, the tunnel ended in a narrow fissure. Trago stepped aside and waved a welcoming hand.

"After you, my friend," he said, "but mind your head on the bookshelf."

Deane first peered suspiciously into the gloomy slit in the rock wall, then ducked his head and squeezed through it. He found himself facing a panel of uncured lumber which stood only a few feet from the rock wall from which he emerged. The wooden barrier narrowed to his left until it was flush with the stone; to the right, it ended abruptly in a hanging cloth curtain of a thick velvet material.

"Please," urged Trago as he exited from the fissure into the cramped space, "go on past the curtain."

Deane did as Trago suggested, parting the dark maroon fabric and stepping past it into the comfortable chamber where the hermit lived.

It was a small entry room, with the mouth of the cave recessed in a wall just opposite Deane. He entered the chamber from behind a high bookshelf stacked with hundreds of old leatherbound volumes and faded magazines. The shelf was cleverly situated so that it hid the tight passage from the fissure which led, in turn, to the magnificent ritual chamber.

A small, heavy, handmade table and bench faced another fissure to the right of the main entrance. The long crack served as Trago's fireplace, and its sides were caked with layers of sooty grease from years of cooking over open fires. The hermit's cot was a neat mattress on a raised frame against the wall next to the bookshelf.

The hermit nodded toward the table. "Sit at my table and share my food, scholar." He did not need to repeat the offer. It had been twelve hours or more since Deane had eaten, and he was famished. Trago served him a bowl of thick stew from the heavy iron kettle hanging over the coals in the natural chimney. The stew was made with a greasy meat, perhaps wild goat, and contained a variety of vegetables. Deane ate the delicious meal in rapid spoonfuls, pausing only to gulp icy mountain spring water from a battered blue metal cup.

"What is it you wanted to show me?" asked Deane when his hunger had abated enough to permit words between mouthfuls.

Trago crossed the chamber to the bookshelf. In the lamplight, Deane could see him fumbling on a shelf among some small items hidden in shadows. He finally located whatever he wanted and returned to the table.

"Have you ever seen anything like this before?" he asked Deane, handing him a highly polished jade figurine. Its milky green surface glistened richly in the soft light, and its dense weight was comfortable in his hand. The beauty of the small sculpture was flawless.

It was one of the familiar Olmec werejaguar designs Deane had seen in museums and illustrations—a human head peering from the jaws of a jaguar, whose claws had replaced the werejaguar's fingers and toes. The breast and stomach of the creature were carved to represent its internal organs that numbered two or four of everything—four lungs, two stomachs, and so on—but only one heart!

"It's Olmec, just like the altar and the stelae," Deane muttered, "and it's the finest I've ever seen. There's not a trace of erosion or excavation scratches. Where did you find this piece, Trago? It's priceless!"

The Indian shook his head slowly. "They are not of 'Olmec' origin, scholar. They are Zoque. I only know of one group of people who called themselves 'Olmec.' They were Aztec castoffs who came to Zoque country very recently as poor fishermen. Their name means "rubber tree people" because they live in the swamps where the rubber trees grow wild. None of them possessed the skills needed to produce such fine sculptures."

Deane held up one hand and nodded impatiently. "I know that the name 'Olmec' was chosen because some of the best sites were located in the swamps where those latecomers lived up until the twentieth century. Archeologists distinguish between the 'modern' and the 'classic' Olmec. Those 'rubber tree people' you mentioned are the modern ones, and we know they had nothing to do with such carvings as these. I'm not going to argue with you about the use of a name, Trago!"

"Forgive my rudeness, scholar," Trago begged. "It is a great surprise to me that you have still not grasped the full truth of what you have seen and heard during the past twenty-four hours. Now I understand why you seem so confused about the Wall."

"Do you mean the 'truth' about the real Olmec? The fact that the people we saw in the temple-cave were ancient Zoque priests and Huastecan warriors. Is that the 'truth' you're talking about?"

Trago smiled delightedly. "You have almost managed to deduce it, scholar. When the Huasta came to our land, they had neither women nor gods. Within a year, they had taken both from us, and made Zoque men like my father their slaves. It was then that I first used the Wall to escape their cruelty."

Trago's mention of Huastec fitted logically with Deane's discovery of Huastec words in the dialect which both Trago and Aruca spoke, as well as that used by the priests and warriors in the cavern.

"And that was how you discovered that the Wall is some kind of dimensional gate which allows you to travel through time," Deane suggested tentatively.

"Not exactly," Trago replied in a harsh whisper. "I owe that discovery to my dear sister."

Deane noticed a sinister tone, perhaps even a note of hatred, when Trago referred to Aruca. His head was reeling with the various bits of Trago's incredible story. He was trying to make them fit the other pieces of the puzzle, especially the tampered computer program, the stories of 'Starmen,' and the source of the Wall. But, more than anything else, he wanted to know more about Aruca and her incredible transformation into a jaguar.

"I'm not sure what to believe just now, Trago. Just

before we entered the Wall, you mentioned something about following your sister through the Mists. What did you mean by that?"

For the first time, a cautious frown darkened the hermit's hawkish face. He bowed his head, then slowly reached for the werejaguar figure.

"Do you understood what this carving represents?" he asked, extending the jade statuette in his open palm to Deane. The linguist took the figure from Trago and turned it so that the lamplight shone on every delicate line of the symbolic sculpture.

"A little," he replied. "My teachers have told me that figures like these represent an Olmec—'Zoque,' that is—cult. I've read of other statues in which humans are portrayed mating with jaguars and having offspring who are neither cats nor people but a mixture of the two. This design represents one of those hybrids."

"Excellent," Trago murmured. "It amazes me to learn how close to the truth your archeologists have come. It is indeed Zoque, and it does represent the cult of the werejaguar!"

"I suppose that you will now tell me that your sister is one of those cat creatures," Deane added wryly.

"But, of course," replied Trago, looking mystified at Deane's amazement. "You see, scholar, you still know very little of my people's history. When the Huastec conquered Talzok, they had no priests of their own. My people worshipped the gods of the jungle, including Chan, the jaguar deity. The Huastec warriors forced our own holy men to serve them, and many devout Zoque men and women turned against the priests."

"What does that have to do with Aruca and her 'disease?'" Deane snapped, having the feeling Trago was avoiding the subject.

"Be patient and let the story unfold," chided Trago. "The priests became more corrupt than ever in the service of their new masters. They ruled with the power of Huastecan spears behind them. On some holy days, they might sacrifice as many as a thousand of their own people on stone altars like the one you saw in the cave!"

"Why did the Zoque permit this to happen?" Deane interrupted, shocked. "Surely they fought the priests?"

Trago smiled sadly. "Do not judge religions you do not understand, scholar. Long before the Huastec arrived, we Zoque practiced human sacrifices. In those days, we believed that a human life was the most magnificent gift we could offer to our gods. The priests who served the Huastec conquerors so cruelly were not doing anything so very different, according to our customs. It was the numbers of their victims that angered followers of Chan."

"So the jaguar cultists rose against the Huastec?"

"Not at first," Trago replied. "They began as small groups of frightened worshippers, who escaped the Huastecs by running into the mountains near Talzok. It was here, in this very cave, that they discovered the Wall."

The old man's story was beginning to sound more coherent. For the first time, Deane felt he was learning something which might help explain what had happened to him and Faranza.

"Then the Wall is directly related to the jaguar cult and to Aruca's transformation?" he asked, trying once again to redirect the hermit's tale toward the Indian woman.

"Of course," Trago said quickly, "but that is only a minor part of the story. No one knows which of the followers of Chan was the first to enter the Wall, but somehow it happened, and that first hero returned with new weapons and dangerous knowledge. Within a few years, news of the Wall reached many ears, including mine. It was said to contain such powerful magic that only the strongest-willed among us could survive traveling through the Mists."

"You mentioned 'new weapons and dangerous knowledge,' Trago. What do you mean? What were these things?"

"I myself saw a small implement now called a 'pistol' which fired a stream of light instead of a projectile. The beam of light possessed the heat of the sun and could burn a hole through the thickest tree at any distance. The man whom I saw using the light-pistol could kill a bird flying at any height with it!"

"And you saw this yourself?" Deane demanded. He was beginning to become absorbed in the hermit's story. It was unlikely that Trago, with his outdated though excellent Spanish, had ever heard of a laser, yet it seemed that he was describing some kind of similar beam-weapon.

"As clearly as I see you," Trago replied in a hushed voice. "But that was only part of the treasure brought from the Wall. There were many strange devices and pieces of clothing no one had ever seen before. And then there were the Starmen themselves!"

" 'Starmen'!" Deane exclaimed. "Describe them! What did they look like?"

"They came from the Wall," Trago replied impatiently. "Dark-skinned men and women wearing round helmets that made them invulnerable to our spears. And others with pointed beards of copper hair like yours! Those were the ones we thought were gods, like Shutec and Yopi. Some of them stayed among us, while others left again through the Wall."

Deane was silent. He was remembering the various Olmec sculptures he had seen, especially the huge stone heads with their football helmets and "African" faces. He also recalled the relief carvings on walls and stelae of slen-

der, beak-nosed men with pointed goatees and huge helmets with many strange designs. Olmec sculptures had
just appeared from nowhere around three thousand years
ago, without any hints of their origin, and the physical
appearances were unlike any that had ever been seen in
Central America before or since that time.

"It was one of the Starmen's machines that taught the
followers of Chan to take the shape of the Jaguar God himself," Trago said, pulling Deane's thoughts back to Aruca.
"I saw it happen only once, just before Aruca joined the
cult called the 'Children of Chan.' The Starmen's machine
was a small, dark blue cube made of a glassy substance.
The cult had made a place for it in the temple-cave, near
the same black altar you saw. It spoke to them without
words, as if their thoughts were one. Whatever was in the
mind of one cultist suddenly appeared in the minds of all."

"A telepathic device!" Deane muttered.

"Perhaps, but it doesn't matter," said Trago. "It was the
Blue Cube which kept many of us from joining the cult of
Chan. We did not like for our thoughts to be open to every-
one. That is a dangerous thing in evil times."

"So you refused to join the cult, but Aruca and others
remained," Deane said.

"Yes," Trago replied sadly. "I think it was one of the Starmen who taught the others the spell to change into the image
of their god, Chan. However they learned it, the Children of
Chan became the Zoque's secret army against the Huastec.
Aided with the strange weapons from the Wall, they waged a
guerrilla war against the invaders. The Huastec, renegade
priests, soon learned that the Zoque's power was derived
from the Wall. They sent many soldiers to the cave to keep the
Children of Chan from using it."

"Then the priests that we saw, Cizin and Enul, were
tools or spies of the Huastec warriors?"

"Exactly," said Trago. "The warriors stay near there, hoping to prevent Chan cultists like Aruca from escaping into the Wall. Each week, they send raiding patrols into the swamps and jungles to capture the Children and bring them back for the sacrifices. Eventually they hope to kill all of the jaguar-people."

"But you and Aruca found your way here, three thousand years later!" Deane protested.

"My sister did manage to escape," said Trago smoothly. Deane was almost positive that Trago was lying about his sister and her "disease," but he could not imagine why.

"I learned about her daring feat from one of the cult's most famous priests, one who spent most of the day in the form of a jaguar. Aruca was one of many who was sent through the Wall to bring help for her people. Travel in the Wall is unpredictable. Unless you have been to another time before, you cannot control where you will stop. That is what happened to Aruca when she came to this place."

"How did you track her?" Deane asked dubiously.

"By deliberately stopping every hundred years or so and exiting the Wall," Trago answered. "If the people I found living here in that new time had knowledge of humans who became jaguars, I tracked my sister in those places. It has taken me more than sixty normal years to reach this place, because I have had to search so many different places. I almost had her cornered when she used the spellwords of the Starmen and escaped me.

"Then the Spanish you speak—"

"—was taught to me by nineteenth century missionaries at Monte Azul," Trago finished. "I spent four years tracing a werejaguar in these very mountains. It proved to be a monk from the monastery below, and I lived there among them long enough to learn that Aruca was elsewhere."

"How long have you been in these hills?" Deane asked.

"In this time period . . . my time period, I mean."

"It took me nearly seven years of your time to find Aruca's trail again," he said. "I first went too far and discovered that a female werejaguar had vanished near Monte Azul some years before. Then I returned in time until I located Aruca in the hills near Kaktunque."

"Then why did you respond so violently in the cantina when you heard my recording?" Deane demanded. "You knew she was here and what she was doing—"

Trago smiled and shrugged.

"When I heard her spell of changing on your machine, I thought that you were a Huastecan spy sent from Talzok to capture us both," he replied. "Hurrying to the cave to see if the Wall had been disturbed, I detected a change in its flow just as you and your companion must have somehow entered the Wall through the device you call a 'computer.' "

Deane shook his head. "You know more than that, Trago. Someone tampered with a game program on the computer and triggered whatever happened to Faranza and me. Who was it that broke into my software, Trago? Was it you?"

The hermit shook his head vigorously. "I told you I know nothing of these machines, nor of sending you into the past! Why would I want to do such a thing?"

"I don't know," Deane admitted, after a moment's hesitation. "But you're the most knowledgeable person I've met since it happened, and it took a sharp somebody to rewrite that program."

"Once again, it was not I," said Trago. He stood up. "I would like to argue with you some more, but I must try to find Aruca before she changes again. She has been gone since you saw her at the ruins. You frightened her away, you see, and accidentally ruined my most careful trace."

"Now wait a minute," Deane objected, grabbing for

Trago's shoulder. "Before you go through the Wall again, tell me how to get my assistant and my machine back here."

Trago scowled, then relaxed suddenly in Deane's strong grip. "The secret of the Wall is concentration. You must block all other thoughts from your mind and think only of your destination. If you have been to a place before, it is easy to recall it and to return there almost instantly once you are inside the Mists. To reach an unknown place, you must try to empty your mind of everything except the thought of traveling forward or backward in time.

Deane shook his head. "I need more information, Trago. Tell me exactly how to find the temple-cave again!"

The hermit's eyes narrowed. "I cannot tell you that, scholar!" he insisted. "But let me resume my search for my sister and then I shall return to help you find your companion and your machine. Give me two days. It will take you at least that long to learn how to bend the forces of the Wall to your will."

Steven Deane has just listened to an incredible story. He must now make an important decision. First, he must decide whether he believes Miguel Trago's version of what happened to him. All other decisions are based on that.

If Steven Deane decides that he believes Trago's story, but doesn't necessarily trust him, he can: make up his mind to travel through the Wall of Mists alone—*turn to page 165*. Or he can try to force Trago to take him back into the Wall, hoping to recover his computer and his assistant—*turn to page 171*.

If Deane decides he believes Trago's story and trusts him to keep his word, he can wait for him to return and take him back through the Wall of Mists—*turn to page 188*.

If Steven Deane decides Trago is lying to him for some reason, he can decide to tell him so—*turn to page 196*.

"I don't want to leave the computer here unguarded," said Deane, "but I also think it would be foolish for us to separate under these circumstances. The only thing we can do is go with them and take the equipment with us."

Faranza nodded toward the hidden chamber. "That place is probably too damp for such a delicate machine, anyhow. Come on, I'll help you carry it out of here."

Once more, Deane was glad he had hired the strong Mayan. The large marine battery which powered the portable computer was heavier than ten of the small consoles, but Faranza could lift it easily. The sculptor pointed to the clay lamp on the floor.

"Give me that lamp and I'll start bringing the equipment while you watch our friends out there."

Deane almost agreed, then remembered that the Mayan had little respect for the delicacy of machines. "Let's both do it," he replied diplomatically. "They're much too afraid of that glowing wall to cross it. In fact, I think that if we had food and water, we could stay here indefinitely."

Retrieving the lamp, Deane made his way along the secret corridor until the pulses of red light from the cracked doorway were too faint to penetrate the thickening darkness. Then, shielding the lighter with his body, he lit the wick of the crude lamp. Its fuel of rancid fat sizzled and stank for a moment or two before bursting into a smoky yellow flame. The acrid fumes forced Deane to stifle a sudden cough. As he paused in the close passage, Faranza pushed past him into the chamber, headed straight for the table with the computer.

"I'll get the machine, Luis!" Deane said quickly as soon as he saw the burly Mayan reaching for the console. "You get the battery."

Deane collected the battery cable and diskette from the cache by the wall. While Faranza was getting the battery from the cavern floor, he folded the screen down over the top of the console's face and stowed the cable in the rear storage compartment of the casing. Then he slipped the diskette into one of the two drive slots, just to protect it on the trip to the warrior's town of Talzok, wherever that might be.

"Ready?" he asked Faranza.

The sculptor was standing by the entrance to the passage, the heavy marine battery cradled in his massive arms as if it were an empty plastic lunch box.

"Whenever you can bring that light over here," he snapped irritably. Deane looked at the Mayan quickly. Moody and erratic, but ordinarily easygoing, Faranza now looked strained and tense.

"Well," thought Deane, "this weird situation is enough to make anyone tense. Faranza looks like he's actually holding up better than I am!"

Grabbing the compact computer by its metal carrying strap in one hand and the small clay lamp in the other, Deane pushed past Faranza and entered the tunnel, the lamp raised in front of his chest to light their way. At the end of the corridor, he blew out the flame and placed the smoldering pot beside the wall. Then he nodded to Faranza and pushed on the rock slab.

The secret portal slid smoothly away from the entrance to the inner passage. Deane could see the warriors peering toward the Wall of Mists. Their refracted view through the thick panel of light would distort the image just enough to heighten the illusion of two "gods" emerging from a solid stone wall.

Faranza pressed against the slab with his back, sealing

the opening without being noticed by the warriors. He then followed Deane through the throbbing barrier of lighted mists. Deane paid little attention this time to the sudden flare and the clouds which hid them briefly from their amazed audience on the opposite side. Seconds later, they were standing in front of the altar with their modern equipment resting on the bloodstained stone surface.

Deane expected the rural Indians to be totally mystified by the portable computer, even though it was packed for travel. He was not prepared, however, for their over-whelmed reaction to the big blue marine battery.

"Look! The Blue Cube of the Starmen!" one exclaimed in a hushed whisper, pointing at the battery.

"It must be the same one given to the Children of Chan!" cried another fearfully. "The Zoque gods are making war on us!"

Scowling, Arras moved to stand in front of the altar, his hands raised high. "Remain calm, spearmen of Huasta! Do not challenge the power of these Zoque gods. Let us know their intentions before we react foolishly, like children afraid of the dark!"

Arras's followers bowed to the two strange beings at the altar, but more than half of them cast nervous glances at the blue plastic battery. Deane was bursting to ask either Arras or Cizin about the "cube of the Starmen" but he dared not risk asking questions that would reveal his ungodly ignorance of such important issues.

"Send me your two strongest warriors!"

Startled, Deane jerked his head toward Faranza, who had issued the terse command to Arras in excellent Zoque-Huastec. Deane had assumed that the Mayan was having difficulty with the mixed dialect because he had remained so silent. But now, the sculptor suddenly revealed a remarkable control of the archaic patois.

117

Faranza did not seem to notice Deane's surprise. Instead, he stared coldly at the two muscular fighters whom Arras had selected. They knelt at the altar, awaiting the god Yopi's pleasure.

"You will bear the Sacred Cube to Talzok," Faranza commanded, "and you will always be remembered for your services. Henceforth, you both will be called 'Guardians of Yopi,' and will be honored as my personal bodyguards and servants!"

Deane watched in total amazement while Faranza's new personal servants virtually swooned at the news of their appointed servitude. He was even more astonished at the change in the sculptor's demeanor. Faranza was absorbing the warriors' adulation as a sponge soaks up water!

Deane frowned when the Mayan finally glanced his way, the strongest signal of disapproval he could risk in full view of the faithful. But Faranza stared blankly at Deane, as though he couldn't imagine what was wrong. Then, turning back, the big Mayan peered out at the throng of warriors.

"Where is Cizin?" he demanded coldly.

"Here, Lord Yopi!" the terrified highpriest exclaimed. "How may I serve you, Skyfather?"

"You can show us the way back to Monte Azul or Kaktunque," Deane started to say, but Faranza interrupted.

"You and Enul will fetch the offerings which these noble warriors have delivered to your gods. The Lord Shutec and I will take the meat with us to Talzok, but you will carry it because you sought to steal it for yourselves in the name of the gods!" Faranza pointed to the two bloody baskets of meat on the altar.

Cizin gave both "gods" a bitter look. He had suffered much humiliation during the past few hours. But he dared not balk at the orders, nor express any beliefs he might harbor that these two were false deities, not in front of these militant believers!

"Enul!" Cizin called gruffly.

His face pale and sick-looking, the fat cleric waddled forward unsteadily to take his load of the meat.

"This has gone far enough!" Deane thought angrily.

"Wait!" he told Enul, then he turned to face Faranza. "That man's just had a heart attack, Luis!" Deane snapped, whispering in English. "He can't carry that basket. It must weigh more than a hundred pounds!"

Faranza's facial expression never changed. He stared coldly at a point somewhere over Deane's head. "He must be punished, Steven," he replied in an flat, cruel tone. "Let's not argue with each other, 'Great Shutec.' It wouldn't be wise for these warriors to see their gods fighting. You better concern yourself with what those spearmen are doing to your precious machine!"

Alarmed, Deane turned away from his confrontation with Faranza just in time to stop the half-dozen hands reaching for the slender computer console. "Mortal hands may never touch Shutec's silver box!" he warned hurriedly. "Its power is divine. It can destroy mere humans in the blink of an eye!"

The threat was effective. His would-be servants backed away in fear of the sinister little case. Arras signaled for the spearmen to leave first, then followed them into the corridor. The two priests stumbled after the warriors, straining beneath the bags of meat. Enul's face was red and splotchy, and sweat was streaming down his cheeks. Deane waited until the two clerics were out of earshot before stopping Faranza at the tunnel entrance.

"What is all this, Luis?" he demanded in English.

"What do you mean?" the sculptor retorted coolly.

"I mean this 'tyrant god' routine!"

"I am merely acting my part," Faranza said, his lips curled in a grim smile. "They think I am Yopi, the ancient Olmec god of new life. You may have forgotten that Yopi, or 'Xipe' as the Mexica called him, was one of the bloodiest gods in ancient Mexico. His priests even dressed in the flayed skins of humans sacrificed to Yopi! No, Steven, they expect me to be cruel. I shall not disappoint them!"

Ducking his tall figure, Faranza entered the passage which led to the cavern's entry chamber. Deane felt a chill run the length of his spine. What Faranza had said was true, but the sculptor seemed to be enjoying this sudden opportunity to play the cruel "god" just a bit too much!

The tunnel exited through a narrow fissure into a cramped chamber. Deane could see the main entrance to the cavern just across from the slit which opened into the torchlit entry room. The rest of the procession was waiting for the two gods outside the mouth of the cave on a wide ledge. When they joined the others, Deane got his first glimpse of their surroundings.

"My God!" he muttered in English, unable to believe his eyes.

The cave exited on the steep side of a mountain that overlooked a valley almost identical to the one where the town of Monte Azul now existed. The stream running through the middle of the valley twisted in different patterns from the Rio Negras which flowed past Monte Azul, but other than that, the topography was nearly identical.

But there was no town!

Deane turned to see if Faranza had noticed this strange occurrence, but the sculptor was walking quickly to catch up with the procession headed along the rim trail. Faranza had not even glanced around, nor—seemingly—noticed anything unusual.

"Maybe there isn't anything unusual," Deane thought disjointedly. "Maybe I'm dreaming—or crazy!"

Shaking his head, Deane straggled at the end of the long procession which wound its way single-file along the precarious mountain path skirting the highest ridge. He walked just behind Enul, who was stumbling forward under the great weight of the bloody basket. Trying to keep a grasp on reality, Deane forced his confused senses to study every detail of the slope, trying to identify his surroundings.

He noticed the blue and green pebbles beneath their feet—the loose serpentine and jade fragments which gave "Monte Azul," or "Blue Mountain," its name. He was definitely in that small cluster of craggy hills that formed part of the large Tuxtla mountain range in the original Olmec heartland.

He kept seeing features which he almost recognized, then some slight difference between them and the images he remembered made him distrust his memory. Suddenly Deane saw the giant mushroom boulder he always used to mark the village of Kaktunque from the road below. There was no mistaking the huge tortoise shell formation on its wind-carved stalk. It was standing, as always, on the very edge of the cliffs which overlooked Kaktunque. The only things missing were the road and the village itself!

Deane was in a daze as he passed by the familiar rock. The jigsaw pieces had rushed together too fast, only to form a larger, more complex puzzle. As he stumbled along the trail, he began to recognize the more permanent features around him, such as the shape of mountain peaks on the horizon and the outline of the distant valley walls. Everything else had changed—fields, towns, villages, even forests and rivers!

The flood of impossible events during the past several

hours, beginning with his witnessing an old woman's changing herself into a jaguar, suddenly swamped Deane's sanity. Reality was no longer a tangible, constant thing. It had become ethereal and mutable. He was living in a place and time that had existed three thousand years before he was born! The sky around him began to swirl dizzily. His feet slipped at the side of the trail as he lumbered along like a sleepwalker.

Just then, the fat priest fell in front of him. The bloody hunks of tapir flesh spilled over the edge of the trail, tumbling hundreds of feet down the steep slope. Deane's stupor cleared instantly. Recovering his own footing, he ran to where the priest lay, face-down in the middle of the trail.

Enul's eyes were wide in fear, and he clutched at his flabby chest and throat, unable to breath. The feathered headdress was crumpled beneath his face where his tongue protruded thickly from his mouth.

"Another heart attack!" Deane shouted in English. "Faranza, come help me!"

Deane heard Faranza ordering the warriors and Cizin to march on ahead, but he didn't pay much attention. Rolling the priest onto his back, Deane was preparing to give the fat man CPR for the second time when Faranza appeared at his side.

"Help me get him away from the edge of the trail," Deane ordered the sculptor without looking up. When the Mayan did not move, Deane glanced around at the giant. Faranza regarded him with a look that was cool, almost pitying.

"You are not strong enough to be a god among these people, my friend. Poor Shutec."

Faranza's kick landed without warning on the side of Deane's head. Grabbing desperately at the Mayan's leg, Deane caught another terrible blow in the middle of his chest. This time, the force of the kick sent him sprawling over the edge of the narrow path, tumbling down the side of the cliff.

Deane clutched in panic at the flimsy roots of the mountain shrubs growing on the steep slope, only to feel them tear out of the rocky soil.

"Faranza!" Deane gasped, seeing the man's face, twisted in a cruel smile, staring at him over the edge of the cliff. Then he was falling . . .

Fish. Someone was cooking fish. Deane opened his eyes. He was lying in a murky room with a haze of stale cooking smoke hanging over his cot. He tried to sit up, only to experience a wave of vertigo and an excruciating pain in the back of his neck. Moaning, he dropped back to the taut surface of the hide litter.

"Mother! He's awake!"

The excited voice of a young boy was so shrill that Deane winced and clamped his hands over his ears. It seemed that the child was screaming inside his skull. Glancing around, Deane tried to recall some small detail of the past which might provide a clue to his location, but could not summon a single image from his befuddled brain.

He heard the slapping sound of running sandals on a hard floor and twisted his stiff neck painfully toward it. In the dim smoky light of the unfamiliar room, he saw a heavy-boned Indian woman approaching his cot. The expression on her broad face was one of fearful concern.

"Where am I?" he tried to say, the words slipping weakly from his dry, cracked lips. The woman's large brown eyes tensed. She recoiled from the bedside and called to her child.

"Run to Arras, Pelon! Tell your father to hasten home.

Tell him that Shutec has awakened and is speaking words of the gods which I cannot understand!"

The woman was issuing the instructions to her son in the ancient Zoque-Huastec dialect spoken by the Olmec, but Deane did not know that. Amnesia seldom affects one's ability to understand or speak languages, and the linguist's case was no exception. He understood everything the woman had said, but made no connection between her ancient speech and his own English words.

"Gods?" he thought, very confused. "What gods? Is my name Shutec?"

"W . . . water," he managed to murmur in the ancient language. "Bring water."

His weakened neck muscles were not even strong enough to turn his head toward the woman. She hurried from the murky chamber, but Deane could still hear her in the next room, fumbling with utensils he guessed were pots.

Within a few minutes, she had returned to his bedside with a wide-mouthed clay jar filled with cool water. The woman dipped her hand in the liquid and bathed Deane's parched lips and sweaty face.

"Drink!" Deane mumbled, raising a trembling hand for the vessel. "Please . . . drink!" he begged weakly.

The woman placed the clay jar against the Deane's lips. He swallowed in great gulps, revelling in the sensation of the cool liquid passing down his parched throat.

"Not too much, Modotl!" warned a man's voice from the door. "You know the wrath of Yopi. If Shutec dies under our roof, Yopi will wear the flayed skin of our son, Pelon, at the next crescent!"

"But he asked me for it, Arras!" she cried. "I only gave him a trickle, as we have done for three moons. Lord Shutec himself ordered me to pour water into his mouth."

The flurry of words confused Deane. His amnesia lifted slightly, allowing him to recognize the names of Yopi and Arras, but only as names of people he once knew. He wanted to see the man's face, hoping that it would jostle a block of his memory into place, and tried once more to raise his head. The pain mounted to a paralyzing cramp which forced him to relax against the hide litter.

"Don't try to move, Lord Shutec," said the man named Arras. "You have not used your muscles in nearly four months, since you left the Cave of the Wall. My wife, Modotl, has kept your human body alive and clean until your spirit chose to return to it."

Wall! Deane's empty mind clutched at the word, sensing something important about it. An image of a red gelatinous mass with an inner pulsating light teased him at the edges of his consciousness, but the dazed scientist could not focus upon it. His eyes closed as fatigue rolled over his entire body. He was vaguely aware of Arras's voice in the room.

"Sleep again, Lord Shutec. Rest so that you will be prepared to hear of your brother's terrible madness."

The next time he was awake, Deane was more alert. Modotl, who had nursed the unconscious "god" for more than a hundred days, brought wash cloths and a small bowl of fish soup to his bedside. He was able to sip Modotl's broth from the bowl without her help. The once athletic scientist began tensing and relaxing his muscles to restore their tone.

Arras entered the chamber just as Deane was managing to sit up in bed for the first time since he awoke.

"Let me help you, Lord Shutec!" he exclaimed, hurrying to put his strong hand behind Deane's shoulder blades. Deane permitted the powerful man to adjust his position on the cot. Then he stared at the muscular Indian, desperately urging a submerged memory to surface.

"You're a warrior!" he said suddenly. "I remember something about spears and blood!"

"I am Arras, Commander of the Huastecan army which captured this sacred city of Talzok three generations ago," he replied proudly. "My grandfather led the Huasta into this swamp and stormed the Zoque citadel. My mother was the firstborn daughter of his noble Zoque concubine."

But the warrior's words meant little to the amnesic scientist. He shook his head in throes of frustration, bringing on a spasm of pain in his neck. Arras leaned forward to help support his weight, but Deane waved him away.

"I'll be all right. Just tell me how I got here. Tell me what you know of me."

The warrior looked amazed. "But, Lord Shutec, I am not a priest! You cannot expect me to know about the lives of gods, especially your own."

For some forgotten reason, Arras's use of the title "Lord" offended Deane, as did the warrior's constant reference to the linguist as a "god."

"Listen to me," Deane commanded weakly. "You can call me 'Shutec' if you like, because I have no other name, but drop the 'Lord' part of it. Look at me! I'm no god! I'm a starved, weak man who can't even remember who he is!"

The sudden emotional outburst exhausted Deane. He collapsed on the cot. Arras bowed to him.

"I will do as you wish. Yopi warned us that you might be insane if you ever awakened."

"Who the hell is this 'Yopi?'"

"Why, Yopi is your brother, Lor . . . Shutec," Arras corrected. "Yopi, the Terrible One, ruler of the dead and of all new life."

"Where is he?" Deane demanded. "If I have a brother,

I want to meet him!"

"Lord Yopi lives in the priests' quarters at the Temple," Arras replied. "He no longer walks the streets of Talzok because the cult of Chan, the Jaguar God, has sworn to destroy his human body."

"And my brother fears these jaguar people?" Another sleeping memory stirred in Deane's clouded brain. "So my brother told you I might be insane if I ever woke up, heh. How did I 'go to sleep,' Arras?"

"You haven't moved since you fell from the steep trail outside the Cave of the Wall," he replied.

Arras's words produced an immediate sensation of falling in Deane's mind. He was crashing headlong down a steep slope, feeling the sharp stones tear into his flesh and bruise his body. Suddenly a rock ledge loomed from nowhere.

"I remember falling!" he exclaimed. "I don't remember anything else, but I recall crashing down a mountainside and—"

Arras nodded. "If you had not struck the ledge, Shutec, your human form would have been crushed on the valley floor thousands of feet below the trail. Lord Yopi told us that your spirit was gone from the body you had borrowed, but that we were to keep it alive and clean in case you wanted to return to it. That is when he told us you might be insane, because the human brain might have been damaged in the fall."

Deane strained for another memory that might trigger others, but they all seemed to linger tauntingly just beyond his grasp. "I'm tired, Arras. Let me sleep and try to remember more tomorrow."

The warrior bowed again. "Yes, Shutec. I will send Modotl to you with food and drink." He stood to leave but Deane stopped him with a frail whisper.

"Arras, do not tell my brother that I've awakened. Let me grow strong enough to go to him at the Temple. If his life is in danger from these jaguar cultists, I would not want him to come here."

The warrior's face displayed a flash of anger, but Arras just nodded. "As you desire, Shutec, so it will be done." Then, as the warrior left the chamber, Deane fancied he had seen the hint of a relieved smile in the man's eyes.

Deane's physical recovery from the fall was rapid. Modotl's massages during the long months of coma had prevented total atrophy of his muscles, and her daily bathing had protected his skin from sores and infections. By the end of the first week of returned consciousness, Deane could walk around the other rooms of Arras's house and attend to his own needs.

Arras provided him with a woven breechclout, a mere strip of cloth passed between the legs and then looped over a belt made from a long rawhide thong. The front and back panels of the loincloth hung like a kilt, but left the sides of Deane's buttocks bare and uncomfortable.

"Was I wearing other clothes when I fell from the trail?" he asked Modotl.

"Yes," she replied. "You were dressed as a god. They were torn by the rocks and underbrush, but I have mended them for you."

She left the room for only a few moments and returned with a large basket. The first item she removed was a crushed Panama hat with a colorful Madras band. Deane took the hat from her and stared at it, lost memories battering at the gates of his conscious mind.

Tossing the hat to one side, he grabbed the basket from Modotl's hands. Hurriedly dumping its contents on the dirt floor, he reached for the faded blue denim shirt. He held it quickly in front of himself, his eyes beginning to burn with tears of both joy and sadness. The amnesia was breaking, forcing him to remember who and where he was! He was also remembering the look on Faranza's face as the sculptor kicked him over the precipice of the mountain trail.

When Arras returned that night, Deane was waiting for him, dressed in his patched American clothes. Though the shock of seeing Shutec in his "godly" attire was sudden, the warrior was even more surprised by the expression of cold anger on Deane's bearded face.

"Tell me about things in Talzok, Arras," he commanded. "Tell me of my 'brother,' Lord Yopi!"

The warrior's face clouded. He looked at Deane doubtfully a moment, then suddenly began to talk in harsh, broken sentences. He himself no longer believed that Yopi was a god, but a mortal creature of incredible evil, perhaps a demon! On some feast days, Yopi had slain as many as two and three hundred Zoque slaves! Yopi had another form as well. He would sometimes appear to them as a god, but at other times he would appear as the god Yopi's chief priest. At these times, he made the people call him "Luz." This Luz performed the cruel acts, but always in Yopi's name!

Arras went on and on, detailing cruelties and atrocities until Deane could scarcely stomach the gruesome tale. "Faranza is obviously insane, probably paranoid schizophrenic," Deane realized. "He imagines himself to be both the terrible god, Yopi, and Yopi's bloodthirsty chief priest and prophet, Luz!"

"We Huasta have always lived with death," said Arras solemnly, "but the cruelty of Yopi-Luz has sickened even the most experienced among my warriors. We have seen him flay women and children alive so that he could dress his giant body in their warm skins while he drank the blood from their throbbing hearts!"

The chief Huastec warrior appeared shocked primarily by the senseless nature of the atrocities. Arras himself had participated in cruel tortures and sacrifices, but those had been related to warfare. This was merely the insane slaughter of defenseless slaves, and it had caused the once-devout military commander to hate Yopi-Luz while serving him.

The horror of Arras's story blasted the remaining blockages from Deane's brain. The shock of being trapped in the past seemed remote and small in comparison to the atrocities attributed to Faranza. Deane vividly recalled the day he and the giant Mayan had left the cave in the company of Arras and his warriors, particularly the sculptor's wild-eyed fascination when he spoke of the cruelties of Yopi worshippers. It was horrifying to think of Faranza as a crazed mass murderer and mutilator.

"We've got to stop him!" Deane exclaimed.

"That may be impossible." Arras shook his head, frowning. "He has surrounded himself with bodyguards recruited from the ranks of our strongest fighters, and he has courted the favors of the Zoque priests, increasing their power tenfold. Even Cizin pays him homage, though at first he blamed him for the death of Enul."

"Surely the Zoque people do not worship this murderer of their children and women! Why don't they revolt against him?"

Arras hesitated, then replied, "There are strange stories circulating throughout Talzok these days—stories of assassins who possess the ability to change their forms into the bodies of jaguars. They have sworn to destroy Yopi's human body. It is said that men from the stars have shown these Children of Chan how to do this magic through the use of Blue Cubes like the one you and Yopi removed from the cave."

Deane recalled the nervous reactions among Arras's men to the large marine battery, but he was more interested in the legends of the Starmen and their mysterious Blue Cube. After many months, it seemed that he might be on the verge of understanding Aruca's transformation into a jaguar.

"Have you ever seen a person change in that way?" he asked Arras.

"No, but I have fought werejaguars. They have human heads and faces on the bodies of giant jaguars. It is said that they take the sacred form of Chan, the God of Jaguars, himself!"

"So this cult, the Children of Chan, is the only movement strong enough to resist Faranza's—I mean, Yopi's—reign of terror," Deane mused. "Where's their camp?"

"In the hills, not far from the Cave of the Wall," Arras replied, a pained look suddenly clouding his face. "In fact, they now fight to control the ritual cave."

"You've just given me an idea," Deane murmured. "Would the Children of Chan join forces with Huastec warriors long enough to overthrow Yopi's regime? I know that you've been enemies for some time, but the two sides have a more threatening mutual enemy in Faranza, uh, Yopi."

Arras stared out the window for a long moment. Then he nodded. "It is possible," he agreed, "but only if a powerful god such as Shutec, himself, would talk to everyone concerned."

Deane thought for a minute or two, then clasped his hands. "I have to do something!" he said, more to himself than to Arras. "I'm responsible for unleashing Faranza on Talzok. I'm the one who thought of becoming a god. It was my computer that brought us back here. Someone tampered with that program and used it to transport us into the past . . . "

He stopped himself because he had just thought of a second alternative. They had traveled into the past by way of some unknown computer effect engineered by a malevolent mind. It ought to be possible to repeat the process and try to stop Faranza in an even earlier past, before he went insane! Perhaps the tampered program itself could be used to undo the damage some phantom programmer had already done.

If Steven Deane decides to enlist the aid of the "Children of Chan" cult of werejaguars in order to stop Faranza, *turn to page 137*. But, if Deane attempts to handle the problem with Faranza by using the computer program again, *turn to page 144*.

FARANZA TRANSFORMED

"Faranza is obviously enjoying the thought of being treated as a god by these primitive people," Deane thought, recalling that the sculptor always talked about his Mayan "ancestors" and daydreamed of ancient times as he worked on the fraudulent Olmec sculptures. "Perhaps that's why he started doing the sculptures in the first place," Deane realized, gaining sudden insight into Faranza's character.

Looking at him, Deane saw Faranza's eyes were filled with excitement, perhaps because of having an opportunity to live his fantasy until they found their way back in time to Monte Azul and Kaktunque.

"You go with them," Deane urged the Mayan, "and try to find out where we are. I want to stay behind and work on that computer program. Maybe between us we'll be able to discover both how we got here and how to get home."

Faranza's look of excitement faded. "I don't think we should separate, Steven," he insisted. "We should both go with them, and take the computer along."

Deane shook his head. "No. I want to be sure that at least one of us is free to go for help if the other lands in trouble. It shouldn't take us very long to get to the bottom of this if we split up."

Faranza frowned but, seeing that the linguist had made up his mind and was not going to change it, he mumbled, "As you wish. If I have not returned within two days, follow my trail to this place called Talzok."

Faranza started for the secret door of the tunnel but Deane stopped him. "Hey," Deane whispered, "try to leave some of that meat for me. As soon as you're gone, I

133

can go outside the cave for some firewood. And good luck!"

Faranza nodded but did not smile. Deane was a little puzzled by his dourness, then simply attributed it to fear of being alone in strange surroundings. The Mayan swung the secret door open and stepped into the invisible alcove behind the Wall of Mists. Deane closed the disguised portal behind him, but left it cracked, so that he could watch the events at the altar.

His huge assistant stepped quickly through the glowing barrier, producing the same flash of light as before. The mist clouds thickened, blocking Deane's view of the ritual chamber, but he heard Faranza's deep voice echoing in the cavern almost immediately.

"Behold, men of Huasta! Yopi has returned from the land of the gods to live among you at Talzok. The Lord Shutec will also appear in your city, but he needs to eat mortal food for three days in order to assume full human form."

"Good for you, Luis!" Deane thought, astonished that the Mayan had learned the Zoque-Huastec sounds so well that his pronunciation was perfect. He knew that the sculptor had a better ear for languages than most people, but this time it was remarkable, even for someone with a Zoque mother!

The throng of warriors on the opposite side of the Wall mumbled excitedly in response to Faranza's reappearance. Just as the opaque mists were beginning to settle, a cloth-wrapped parcel sailed through it with another flash of light, disturbing the clouds again. The bulky package landed at the base of the hidden doorway, oozing dark blood from within. Deane did not need to unwrap it to know that the Mayan had tossed him enough fresh tapir meat to last until he could return. All he needed was firewood, and there should be plenty of that just outside the cavern mouth.

From the other side of the cloudy Wall, Deane heard sounds of footsteps and voices diminishing in the distance. When the barrier was finally clear again, he could see that the ritual chamber was empty. Deane waited for several minutes to be sure that the warriors had really gone. Then he stepped cautiously from the tunnel and closed the secret door behind him.

Ignoring the food for the moment, he decided to explore the cavern while the torches were still burning. He lunged through the pulsating transparent panel, shielding his eyes from the now-familiar flash of intense light. In the next instant, the scientist was standing in front of the blood stained altar of heavy basalt.

Before he examined any other detail of the empty cavern, Deane wanted to study the mysterious Wall of Mists which had provoked such great fear in the minds of the seasoned warriors. It had seemed so harmless to him, yet was regarded as a dangerous force by both the priests and their warrior supplicants.

"The first thing to do is to find the source of that energy," he reasoned. "It's bound to be projected from above."

Deane stared at the deep shadows of the cavern's ceiling, encrusted with stalactites and columns extending all the way to the floor. There was nothing that looked like the usual beam of light streaming from the lens of a projector, as he had imagined he would find. Unsatisfied, he stepped closer to the throbbing patch of red light which resembled a thick rectangular layer of luminescent gelatin. Hesitantly, the scientist probed the surface of the patch with his forefinger.

At the moment the tip of his finger grazed the pulsating

---

panel, the entire surface of the Wall flared with a brilliant white light that rose from its red surface like a thin crystalline sheet. The sheet became a pulse of energy that shot upward so fast that Deane could hardly follow it.

The outline of the sheet of pure energy remained as an afterimage against the shadows of the ceiling. Its sides formed the planes of a pyramid of spectral light, with the rectangular base centered at the Wall of Mists and the apex of the four convergent sides located in one brilliant speck of light shining like a bright star above the stone altar.

Turn to page 94.

CAPTURED!

"I want you to arrange a meeting for me with the leaders of the Children of Chan cult, Arras," said Deane. "Using their strength against Faranza and his private army may be our only opportunity to end Faranza's bloodbath."

"Who is this 'Faranza' you keep mentioning, Shutec?" asked the veteran warrior.

" 'Faranza' is your 'Lord' Yopi's real name, Arras. He's no god, and neither am I. My name is Steven Deane, not 'Shutec.' I would try to tell you where we come from, but you'd never believe it. In fact, I'm not sure that I believe it!"

"But you appeared through the Wall of Mists," Arras protested. "I saw you myself! And Yopi-Luz, or whatever his name is, had the legendary Blue Cube of the Starmen!"

The warrior's mention of the "Starmen" refreshed Deane's recovering memory of their re-entry into the ritual cavern, when he had longed to ask someone about the mysterious "Blue Cube."

"That was just a battery for my compu—" he began, then stopped. "Uh, that was a special box I use to . . . Oh, never mind! Who are these 'Starmen,' anyway?"

Arras stared dubiously at Deane, then his face cleared. Apparently he was not fully convinced that the red-bearded creature was a mere man and he did not pretend to understand the strange ways of gods.

"According to some of the Zoque slaves, a man from the stars who took the form of Shutec taught the first Children of Chan how to use the special Blue Cube to change their bodies into jaguars or any other creatures they chose. No one among us has ever seen the Cube, but we thought this 'bat tree' of yours must be the same one."

137

"Well, it isn't!" Deane assured the warrior. "How about these 'Starmen?' Did anyone ever see them besides the original Children of Chan?"

Arras paused for a moment, then shrugged. "I don't think so, Steefandeane." He was running the two names together, but Deane decided not to attempt too much in one day. Ridding himself of "Shutec" was enough of an accomplishment. As for the "Blue Cube" and the "Starmen," the legend of the Chan cultists was beginning to sound like some "visiting-gods-from-space" story.

"All right." Deane paused, then, "Where is *my* Blue Cube from the cave now?" he asked Arras.

"At Yopi-Luz's temple, with the sacred box you were carrying when you fell from the trail, Steefandeane," he replied. "When you did not recover from the fall, Yopi—uh—"

"Faranza," Deane corrected.

"Faranza took it with him. He keeps it in the place where he makes people from stone."

"People from stone!" Deane exclaimed. "What do you mean? What do they look like?"

"They are huge heads with round warrior's helmets and faces like Yopi-Luz's."

"Oh, that's just carving, Arras. There's nothing divine about those, either." Deane had seen the look of awe in the warrior's eyes and realized that Faranza had been using his sculptural talents to impress these simple people with his "godlike" powers.

"Lord Y—uh, Faranza has taught all the Zoque priests this 'sculpture' thing," said Arras, frowning. "They tell us it is a great and dangerous power!"

"They're lying," Deane replied. "It can be 'great,' but not very dangerous—unless one of Yopi's stone people fell on you."

Arras started to laugh, then suddenly choked, glancing uncertainly at Steefandeane-Shutec. Deane grinned.

"Go ahead! You can laugh if you want to. It was just a little joke."

The warrior's pent-up fears of the gods burst from his tense throat, echoing in the large room. Deane's own tension broke, and the two men of very different times and cultures embraced in a frenzy of laughter which brought Modotl and her son running into the room. Arras and Deane tried to stop their hysterical bellylaughs but could not. The pleasant contagion spread quickly to the woman and boy, who welcomed this rarest of opportunities for humans to laugh with a god.

Deane could barely see the mountain trail in the twilight of dusk. He and Arras had arranged to meet the leader of the cult of the Jaguar God, Chan, at the holy Cave of the Wall just after dark. They had timed their trip so that they would arrive slightly before the cult leader. That way, Arras could remain on guard outside the cave while Deane and the guerrilla chieftain conferred within.

Their plans proceeded without a hitch. Deane squeezed through the fissure which led to the ritual chamber while Arras remained in the shadowy entrance room. Whoever sought access to the inner cavern through the slit would have to pass by the spear and dagger of Talzok's best warrior.

Deane's first view of the chamber brought a rush of memories. From the rear of the cavern, he could see the massive altar of black basalt, glistening darkly in the combined light of several dozen torches and the steady pulses of red light from the mysterious Wall of Mists.

Deane was vaguely conscious of a change in the ritual chamber, but did not grasp it until he started walking slowly toward the altar. It was only as he neared the bloody boulder that he saw the carved columns of limestone which would be called "stelae" by archeologists of the future.

Someone had carved the first three rows of stalagmites into pillars covered with the typical symbols and figures of the "Olmec" culture! Crouching beside the nearest one, Deane studied the designs carefully. There could be no doubt that Faranza had either carved these stelae or had supervised them. They contained the same recurrent emblems and features he had seen the Mayan chisel on dozens of fake "Olmec" artifacts in Kaktunque. As if that were not enough proof of their origin, there was a large pair of parallel lines in base relief centered at the top of the pillar, with a perfectly round dot over them—Faranza's "signature mark," as he had called it in Merida such a long time ago!

Deane quickly surveyed the other stelae, verifying their similar styles and finding the Mayan's mark on each one. Arras had been right about Faranza's sculpting lessons. His former assistant, now self-appointed god and prophet, had taught his priesthood the most durable art of all. The scientist suddenly realized that hundreds of centuries later, the Mayan's work would come to be known throughout the world as the "definitive Olmec style!" He had discovered the long-sought origin of the mysterious Olmec art which would influence all later cultures in Latin America!

He was so absorbed in his fascinating discovery that he did not notice the flare from the Wall of Mists behind the altar. Nor did he hear the stealthy feline steps of a person entering the cavern from the Wall.

"So this is the famous 'Shutec!' "

The voice startled Deane so completely that he lost his footing and fell back against the freshly carved stelae. Towering above him was a slender woman wearing a loose low-cut gown of white cloth beneath her magnificent robe of a giant jaguar skin. The head of the beast had been hollowed and dried so that it fit her own head. A stunning mass of black hair cascaded from the skin hood to lay in loose curls against her smooth, tanned breasts. The jungle cat's claws had been fashioned into mittens which the woman wore on her hands.

"Come now, my 'Lord Shutec,' " she challenged Deane sarcastically. "Gods are not supposed to know fear."

"Who are you? How did you get past Arras?"

"I am Aruca, Priest-sister of Chan," she replied. "You were to meet with me alone, yet I find that you have laid a trap with Huastec spears."

The name of the old woman from Kaktunque, as well as the same title he had translated from Aruca's incantation, stunned Deane.

"I see that you were not prepared to welcome me by way of the Wall of Mists, 'Great Shutec,' " she continued. "How is it that you, who taught my ancestors the Way of Changing as well as that of the Wall, did not expect a Priest-sister of Chan to come through the Wall of Mists?"

Deane recovered his composure, though he was still confused by the woman's name and by her mention of traveling through the Wall. He felt sure that she had simply been hiding in the secret chamber, just as he and Faranza had hidden from the warriors years ago.

"I do not pretend to be a god, Aruca. And the man who guards the entry chamber is Arras, the Huastec chieftain who wishes to unite his forces with the Children of Chan. I commanded him to guard our meeting so that Faranza, or 'Yopi,' cannot interfere with it."

The priestess seemed to be considering Deane's explanations. Finally, she made a noncommittal sound and waved a hand toward the carved pillars.

"Do you know that each human figure on these stones represents a Zoque man, woman, or child whose skin has been ripped from his or her body while they were still alive? Can you imagine the blood that has flowed from that evil black altar at the hands of the giant murderer who now calls himself 'Yopi-Luz' and wears those bloody skins, still warm from their victims' bodies?"

Tears of anguish and hatred filled the priestess's eyes. Deane could see that he would not need to urge the Children of Chan to take up arms against Faranza.

"Then you should agree to the alliance with Arras's Huastecs," he told Aruca. "Together, you can rid Talzok of this crazed demon."

But before the priestess could answer, a flash of light from the Wall caused her to twist around toward the altar. Deane stared in amazement at a towering figure, who stepped from the patch of translucent mists into the ritual chamber. He wore a heavy robe of tanned rabbit skins and had shaved every hair from his oiled head and face. It took Deane several seconds to recognize his former assistant without the thick black eyebrows and moustache.

"Your face betrays your feelings, Steven," Faranza said. "I knew even before we met that you'd lead me to this witch. I just didn't know when. That's why my agents have been watching Arras's house since you were taken there." Faranza heaved a sigh. "I was hoping that you'd simply die so that we might avoid this little scene."

'Before we met!' Deane caught the casual phrase, but did not understand it. "What on earth—"

Ignoring Deane, Faranza turned to the priestess.

"As you can see, Aruca, you are not the only person who can use the Wall to go where or when they choose!"

"YOU DEMON!" yelled the priestess. Flinging herself at the giant, she slashed at his face with the jaguar talons.

142

Faranza stepped aside, dodging her attack, and grabbed her by the waist. Pinning her with his great weight against the bloodstained altar where he had slain so many of her compatriots, he drew a thin blade of obsidian from his cape.

"STOP, FARANZA!" Deane screamed. Lunging across the altar, he punched the mad sculptor in the face. Faranza reeled backward, giving Aruca time enough to kick his unprotected groin and dive headlong into the Wall. Deane saw the blood dripping from Faranza's nose in the sudden flare of light. Hearing noises outside, Deane slammed the sculptor to the rock floor and kicked the black dagger from his hand. Just as he was reaching for the weapon, several pairs of hands grabbed him from behind.

Turn to page 159.

LORD SHUTEC

"Where is the silver box I had with me when I fell from the mountain trail?" Deane asked the warrior.

"In Yopi-Luz's temple," Arras answered. "No one will touch either it or the Blue Cube which came from the Cave of the Wall. You, yourself, warned us never to touch the box, Lord Shutec."

"I'm not a 'Lord' and neither is the one you call 'Yopi-Luz,' " said Deane. "My name is Steven Deane and his name is Luis Faranza. We're humans, just like you are, and those things are harmless unless misused. I just said that to keep curious hands away from my computer."

"What is this 'computer,' Steefandeane?"

"It's a weapon which just might end our problems, Arras," replied Deane, "but I'll need to use it in the Cave of the Wall. Can you get it and the . . . the Blue Cube for me?"

Doubt clouded the warrior's face.

"He probably still thinks of the battery as some kind of weapon given to the Children of Chan by men from the stars—like the Blue Cube they mentioned earlier," thought Deane.

"Come on, Arras!" he urged. "It's our best chance— maybe our only chance—to stop Faranza. Will you do it?"

The Huastec chieftain frowned but nodded. "Some of my men are guards at the Temple. I can still trust a few to do as I say. I shall instruct them to steal the things you need, Steefandeane."

"Good! Have the equipment at the cave by tonight. You can leave it on the altar. We'll end Faranza's reign of terror before the sun rises tomorrow!"

Arras led Deane to the Cave of the Wall just at dusk,

then left him there reluctantly. Deane had finally convinced the warrior to take his family away from Talzok, just in case his plan failed. At least he would have saved three lives from Faranza's cruel madness. After the warrior had gone, Deane ducked into the dark cavern.

He groped his way to the fissure and squeezed through it into the narrow, lighted passage that led to the main chamber. Even from the opposite end of the ritual cave, Deane could see two bulky articles on top of the flat basalt boulder.

He hurried to retrieve the equipment, anxious to see if the battery still had enough power to even start the computer's circuits. It was a heavy duty, sealed battery of the type which "never needed service" according to its advertisements. Deane felt sure that it would not start an automobile engine after remaining idle for six months, but he hoped that it still held the small charge necessary to spark the circuits of the tiny microprocessors inside the computer.

Starting with the heaviest article, he grabbed the large battery and staggered into the Wall of Mists with it. The barrier did not seem to have changed during his long period of amnesia. Predictably, it produced a blast of white energy as soon as he touched it, followed by the misty black-rimmed red clouds which swirled before him and blocked his view of the cave. Without hesitating, Deane took a few more steps and found himself in the niche behind the Wall. He set the battery on the floor and pulled on the slab which hid the tunnel leading to the secret chamber.

The perfectly fitted portal swung away from the opening. Deane saw the small oil lamp on the floor, just where he and Faranza had left it. Before retrieving the battery, he lit the oily wick and waited for the burning animal fat to sputter and settle into a steady flame. Then he placed the lamp on top of the battery and lifted it to his chest.

The straight passage had not changed, either. He followed it to the inner chamber, where he saw the old camp table they had left standing in the center of the room. By the meager light of the oil lamp, he situated the battery on the floor beneath the table and returned to the main cavern for the computer.

As he lifted the silvery case from the altar, he noticed for the first time that there were faint lines slanting upward from the corners of the Wall of Mists. They appeared as ghostly beams of light defining the outermost edges of a pyramid whose base was the glowing Wall itself. The four sides of the pyramid seemed to converge at a lighted apex high above the altar amid the deeper shadows of the ceiling.

Suddenly intrigued by the discovery of what might be the Wall's source of energy, Deane started to look for some way to reach the distant, starlike tip of the pyramid. Then he remembered his more immediate mission and stepped into the Wall with his computer. The flash nearly blinded him this time, because he was backing into the Wall, but he saw a sheet of pure energy streaking upward, inside the nearly invisible pyramid, all the way to the pinpoint of light at the apex!

Puzzled, Deane turned and stepped out of the Wall, then hurried into the passage and made his way in the semi-darkness to the inner chamber. Once there, he quickly attached the cable to both the computer and the battery. Holding his breath, he flicked the voltmeter switch on the front of the console and checked the voltage. It was registering in the "weak" range, but seemed to have enough juice left for one or two good attempts to remedy the current problems with Faranza.

Making sure that the diskette with the tampered game program was still in the drive, Deane pressed the ON key and waited, but nothing happened. He tried again, but with the same results. The disk drive mechanism seemed frozen after half a year of disuse, and may have even corroded during the wet summer months.

Deane felt bitter disappointment wash over him. "Come on!" he muttered to the machine, slapping it lightly. His experience with computer hardware had taught him that a good jarring tap sometimes worked to get a sluggish drive going. This time, however, it did not.

Deane stared at it a moment, then hastily searched his pockets for something he could use to open the console. His fingers first grazed the lighter, then closed over his favorite general tool, the common pocket knife.

"Now we're in business!" he thought. In a matter of minutes, he had managed to loosen the Phillips-head screws which held the console's casing in place and lifted the portable's chassis from the two tiny drive mechanisms.

Deane knew much more about software than hardware, but he could recognize trouble when he saw it. A computer's disk drives, he knew, were the only moving parts of the console and therefore the most likely places for problems to develop. He was expecting to see spots of rust and was hoping to free the small components of whatever corrosion was there.

Surprisingly, both three-inch drive mechanisms were in perfect condition! They were not only entirely free of rust and corrosion, but they still glistened with a fine layer of silicon lubricant applied at the factory. The artificial cave was much dryer than he had thought.

"Damn!" he swore out loud, wondering where the problem might be. Leaning back in the camp chair, he mentally reviewed each step of the computer's operating cycle, trying to use logic to pinpoint the stoppage.

"Let's see," he muttered to himself, "power on, start firmware, firmware fetches system boot, boot loads the operating system, operating system turns drive. The ON switch is lit, which means we've got power, and the drives are fine, so the beginning and the end of the cycle are O.K. But the screen's dead—no messages or anything. If it was a software problem, like the boot or the operating system, I'd get a message. It's got to be the firmware!"

Deane turned the lightweight console around so that he could see the expansion slots in the back, where "boards" of microchips were plugged into the computer. He had installed two of them himself, one huge graphics board and another one with extra memory for the kind of linguistics programs he needed to run. The only other board contained the chips installed at the factory—the machine's "firmware," including the main one, a powerful thirty-two bit DEC microprocessor.

Using the pocket knife to loosen the clamp screws on the slots, he freed the master or "mother" board and removed it from the machine. The scientist tilted the small panel with its hundreds of chips and circuits toward the lamplight to get a better look at it. At first, he thought perhaps he was just not looking at it correctly, but when he examined it more closely, his scalp tingled with a mixture of shock and disbelief. The central processing unit—an assembly that held the master chip—was missing!

Frantically, Deane looked on the table beneath the console, as well as inside the chassis, but the chip assembly had not dropped when he removed the board from the machine. As incredible as it seemed, someone else in this primitive world knew enough about computers to have removed its most essential element!

"And that's bound to be the same person who used the

game program to bring us here!" Deane said to himself. "If I can find the missing chip, I'll have that part of the mystery solved, at least. I might even be able to reverse the effects of the program or force whoever did this to help me do it."

Deane was just replacing the mother board into its slot when he heard a noise. Footsteps! From the entry passage! He bounded from the chair, only to remember that there was no place to hide in the small cubicle of stone. When he could see the flicker of torches approaching the hidden chamber, he called in desperation.

"Arras! Is that you!" For a breathless moment, only silence answered him. Then the corridor was filled with deep-voiced laughter, magnified many times by the megaphone effect of the tunnel-chamber combination. Long shadows spilled into the cubicle seconds before a giant man ducked through the open doorway.

"Faranza?" Deane whispered.

For a moment he did not recognize him. The sculptor had shaved his head completely, including even his eyebrows, and had rubbed some kind of oil or grease all over his face and body. The Mayan wore a rounded hide helmet like the ones on the massive stone heads sculpted by the Olmec. In fact, Faranza's broad, almost African facial features were so similar to those of the carved basalt heads that he might have modeled for them personally.

"So you are alive!" Faranza exclaimed in English, seeing Deane's astonished face in the light of the torches borne by at least ten of his followers, who were crowding into the cramped chamber.

Deane could only stare. Faranza was dressed entirely in native clothing: soft leather loincloth with painted designs, a necklace of beaten gold and human bones, and a fine cloak of bright feathers lined with rabbit fur. The gleaming black blade of an obsidian axe swung at his side, his naked hips and thighs protected from its sharp edge by a strip of leather.

Deane found his voice. "Yes, I'm alive, despite your best efforts to kill me."

"Whatever I did was in the best interests of the people of Talzok!" Faranza claimed. "They did not need a weak Shutec then, and they do not need one now."

"How can you talk about their 'best interests' when you kill their women and children for your own pleasure?" Deane charged. "You're deranged, Faranza! A sick man!"

The Mayan's heavy jowls creased in a smug grin. "No, Steven, it's you who are ill. As everyone knows, your human brain was damaged when you accidentally fell from the trail such a long time ago. There is only one proper treatment for a malfunctioning brain. It must be removed and offered to Yopi by his priest, Luz. You are fortunate that both the god and his priest are here in my body, Steven. We will be able to treat your illness right here in this very chamber."

Deane's throat suddenly became too dry to swallow. He saw Faranza's hand lifting the hatchet of volcanic glass from his side and removing the leather strip. Deane began backing away from the giant and his armed henchmen.

"Stop the Lord Shutec!" commanded the Mayan in the Olmec hybrid dialect. "He has become dangerously insane. See, he has stolen the sacred blue and silver boxes from the Temple and plans to give them to the Children of Chan. I must free him of the injured human brain so that he will be able to seek another. Hold him!"

The guards with Faranza fanned out in the cramped cubicle, forcing Deane into a far corner and wedging him against the wall. Seizing his wrists, they dragged him toward the table with the computer. One of them grabbed the American scientist by his thick golden hair and bent his head backward against the wooden surface.

Faranza approached the table with his obsidian axe raised high above his helmeted head. When he reached Deane's side, the scientist tried desperately to kick him and break away, but the powerful hands held his head and arms too firmly.

"Stop, Faranza!" Deane tried once more. "Help me find the missing part of this computer and we'll be able to return to our own time! There are people who can help you back there!"

Faranza hesitated, peering around the chassis of the console at the loosened mother board.

Deane felt hope swell in his heart, but it vanished with Faranza's next smug words.

"Well, well! You've been busy since you left Arras. How did you know to check the firmware so quickly? I imagined it would take you at least a few days to spot the missing chip."

Deane was too amazed to say anything at all. "I should have realized!" he thought in agony. "Faranza was the only person who could have had access to the computer both before and after we arrived in the past!" He also recalled how the Mayan had tried repeatedly to get his hands on the machine just after they came. He was just beginning to remember other clues linking Faranza to the computer, and to wonder both why and how the sculptor had engineered their travel into the past, when the black blade freed "Lord Shutec" from his "defective" human brain.

THE END

THE DANCE OF THE CATS

Deane could not banish the image of the young priestess from his mind. Memories of her stunning beauty clouded his thinking. He must go back to talk to her, he reasoned. She could explain what had happened to Aruca only a few days earlier. She also, apparently, knew more details about the Wall of Mists and its mysterious effects. Deane told himself that his decision to go back and see her was based on cold logic, but in his heart he knew it was because he wanted simply to see her, perhaps touch her. . . .

Deane circled back through the shadows of the highland forest toward the encampment of the Children of Chan, the Olmec's Jaguar God. The drums and flutes were louder as he crept among the shadows toward the bonfire in the clearing. The fire itself had grown considerably, its flames ascending so high into the night sky that the bright orange and yellow tongues appeared to lick the top branches of huge cypress trees and to blot out the weaker lights of the stars themselves. Deane moved closer until he could see the dancers clearly.

They were all males, the same ones he had seen earlier. Their ragged jaguar pelts tossed and flapped about their sweaty bodies as they jerked in rhythm with the haunting melody. Their movements were sensuous at first, but became frenetic as the drumbeat raced faster. Within several minutes, they were twisting in spasms of what seemed to be either pain or extreme ecstasy, judging from their facial expressions.

Deane crowded closer to try to hear the unintelligible sounds coming from the dancers' throats. At first he thought they were grunts of tension or pain, but soon realized that they were actually snarls and low, rumbling roars. The only time he had ever heard a human make such bestial sounds was three day's before when he had watched the old woman, Aruca, become a jaguar!

Almost fearing what he would see next, but unable to stifle his fascinated curiosity, Deane ran from the leafy shadows of the forest fringe to the rear of a thatched hut made of small logs and sunbaked mud. Pressing his body against the rough timbers, he inched his way toward the corner where he would have a clearer view of the ritual.

As soon as he peered around the edge of the small building, Deane felt his skin grow clammy with a cold sweat. The dancers were neither human nor jaguar, but something between the two! The ragged pelts still hung and bounced from their shoulders, but they no longer covered normal human skin. Bright new fur had appeared on their legs, arms, and chests!

Something was different about their musculature and bone structure as well, but it took Deane a few more moments of stunned watching to discover what it was. Their shoulders and hips had become more angular, while their arms and legs had shortened. They still stood and walked on their hind legs, but it seemed to require awkward movements, as if an entire pack of housecats were dancing on two feet!

It was an eerie, almost comical scene to watch these hideous monsters try to keep in rhythm with the drum and flute music. Deane was gripped by an insane desire to laugh.

The heads of the werejaguars changed less than any other portion of their bodies, but their inhuman qualities were still obvious. A thin layer of mottled yellow and black down covered their foreheads and cheeks, and their noses flattened and merged with their upper lips, becoming muzzles. But it was the eyes that presented the strongest similarities to wild felines. No human eyes could have reflected the firelight in such an incandescent amber hue.

Deane clutched hold of reality firmly, forcing his scientific mind to react to this strange scene with detached, clinical calm. From his memory of Aruca's change, Deane expected to see the men continue their transformations until they were copies of the beautiful Central American jungle cat. But the male werejaguars did not complete the transition from human to beast as the old woman had done. They remained in an awkward nether state, unable to stand fully upright and lacking the boundless feline grace of the cat they worshipped.

The drum and reed music stopped abruptly. The frenzied werejaguars halted their sinuous twisting and growling almost immediately and fell to the ground, panting heavily like any exhausted animal. There was a soundless interval in which Deane began to feel a tinge of excitement. Something was about to happen, he was sure of it.

It began as a low rumble from the throats of the werejaguars lying on the dance ground. Deane recognized the sound from somewhere, but could not place it exactly. Then he had it. They were purring! It was the unmistakable roaring of a contented cat, magnified many times in both volume and bass tones. The soft glow of the huge fire on the half-furred pelts lent an atmosphere of tranquility to the nightmarish scene.

All at once there was a fierce, screaming roar, and then another, from the direction of the musicians' area. Deane's scalp prickled as he saw two of the largest, most beautiful female jaguars he had ever seen slink into the clearing. Both were tremendous cats for their species and sex, just as large as the one he had seen bound from an Olmec altar stone only a few days ago.

The pair of jungle cats roamed among the werejaguars, who were stretched lazily on the ground, basking in the firelight. The females paused occasionally to lick and groom selected male werecats. A few of the males made clumsy attempts to mate with the powerful females, but were driven away with a quick toss of a sleekly muscled neck, or a heavy slap from a paw with sheathed claws. A serious snarl or two was usually enough to keep the aroused male werecats at bay.

While Deane watched the curious scene, the males' fur began to fade and the bodily changes started reversing themselves. One-by-one, the dancers recovered their lithe nude forms and lay sprawled on the ground by the dying bonfire. The twin females continued to pass among them, licking those who had not begun to revert to human form. Soon, all of the dancers had recovered from their transformations and were lying asleep with the filthy skins wrapped around their own naked and sweaty bodies.

The fire dwindled to a gentler level, casting its soft light on the two female jaguars. At first, Deane thought it was a trick of the failing light, but then he realized that they had begun to change, too. The beasts' legs began to lengthen and the magnificent fur became lighter over their human female bodies. The werecat closest to Deane was a slender, youthful woman with muscular legs and firm breasts. Her jaguar's head remained after the rest of her slim human form had returned, marring her beautiful figure. It was the other werejaguar, however, that captured most of Deane's attention. As it changed, the creature developed the sagging flesh and bosom of an old woman! Deane was suddenly back at the Olmec ruins in his mind, watching a reversal of Aruca's astonishing transformation.

He forced himself to gaze upon the two women's faces as they, too, began to resume their human features. The cruel muzzles retreated first, followed by the rounded feline shape of the skull, and then the fur and the eyes. Deane tensed himself, waiting for the moment when he would see Aruca's withered face above the wrinkled body. While their heads were transforming themselves, several of the musicians appeared with fine jaguar pelts and covered both women's nude bodies. It was the addition of the jaguar robes that told Deane their identity.

The old Aruca was not there. This was the young priestess with the same name and her elder companion, both leaders of the Children of Chan movement. The fur had almost vanished from both their faces when Deane received the greatest shock of all. The young woman's face was nearly free of the gold and black markings when a trick of the firelight revealed the bone structure.

"Aruca! It *is* you!" Deane blurted involuntarily. The two priestesses and their servants froze at the sound of his voice. The younger woman recovered immediately and turned on her heels to run.

"Don't go, Aruca!" Deane yelled. "I want to talk to you!"

For the second time in less than a few hours, he saw the terrified expression of a frightened animal on her lovely face. Once more he saw her as a wild creature of the forest fleeing for her life. She darted away from the fire into the deeper shadows of these strange hills.

"Go after her, messenger of Shutec!" said the old woman. "Stop her before she enters the Wall of Mists!"

"The Wall? In the ritual cave?" he demanded. "Why?"

"Hurry! She will outrun you!" That was apparently all the old woman would tell him.

Deane left the dance circle just as the groggy male werecats were realizing that something had happened. Dodging into the undergrowth, he headed straight for the path that had taken him to the clearing from the mountain trail.

He reached the mouth of the cave quickly and ducked

without pausing into the entry chamber, squeezing himself into the slit that opened into the inner corridor of the ritual chamber. From the rear of the spacious cavern, he could see the pulses of red light behind the altar cast a ghostly hue over everything. The Wall had not been disturbed within the past few minutes because it was crystal clear. Aruca had not entered it yet. But where was she?

Deane walked slowly toward the altar, winding his way among the tombstone-shaped stalagmites in the subdued flashes of pink light. He had nearly reached the altar when he heard a low rumbling growl from somewhere in the chamber. His hair prickled on his neck and a shiver convulsed his body. He froze, careful to make no sudden moves as he slowly let his head turn, searching the cave. It was impossible for him to pinpoint the beast's growl because of the distorting echo in the cave. But suddenly he saw a shadow dodge past a column only ten yards away. It was the shadow of a woman, not a beast.

"Listen to me, Aruca!" Deane called desperately. "I have not come to harm you! I want to help you!"

The only reply he heard was another low growl. This time, he was almost positive that it had come from his right. He took a few steps in that direction, peering into the darkness as far as he could. He had just taken another step when a blur of a jaguar pelt and the shimmer of beautiful dark hair flashed behind him, past the edge of the altar. He dived toward Aruca, encircling her slender waist with his arms at the exact instant she touched the lighted Wall of Mists.

Things happened too quickly for Deane to follow for a moment. He was vaguely conscious of his arm around Aruca's waist, but the flash of energy when they struck the Wall distracted him. They struggled, it seemed, but more in a mental than a physical way. It was over almost as quickly as it had begun, with Aruca pushing Deane away from her and bounding out of the Wall, back into the cavern. The thick clouds within the Wall blinded Deane for a moment, but then he managed to stumble into the chamber after her.

Deane realized that something was very different as soon as he stepped toward the altar. The cavern was now brightly lit with flaring torches. Moments before, it had been dark except for the throbbing light of the Wall. Aruca was there, too, but she was not alone. Deane saw her struggling in the grasp of a giant man, whose tanned bald head shone in the flickering torchlight. Two other men stood near the giant's side, both wearing caps of jaguar skin and carrying heavy spears with obsidian tips.

Before the two guards could react, Deane had covered the distance between the altar and the back of Aruca's captor. He plowed into the huge body, striking at the small of the man's back with both fists clenched together.

"DROP HER!" he yelled as he landed a powerful blow.

The big man's knees bent and his shaved head flew back. As he toppled to the floor, Aruca darted out of his weakened grasp and ran for the tunnel at the far end of the cavern. The two guards stared in confusion at their fallen leader.

"Lord Yopi!" one exclaimed, rolling the giant onto his back.

Deane gazed at the man's completely shaven face and head, not recognizing it at first without eyebrows, moustache, beard, or hair. Then the man opened his eyes. Deane gasped.

"Faranza!"

Turn to page 159.

Deane strained but could not free himself from the powerful grasp of the two warriors who were binding his wrists.

"It grieves me to see that you have joined forces with my enemies, Steven," said Faranza in Spanish. "Together, we might have ruled the mightiest empire of this ancient world. You as Shutec, the Fiery One, and I in the dual role of Yopi and his prophet, Luz. Look around you! Do you not see my power and influence here?"

Deane glanced beyond Faranza's towering figure into the brightly lit ritual cavern. Freshly carved stelae were everywhere, their intricate symbols gleaming in the torchlight. Deane suddenly understood one of the more incredible aspects of the sculptor's insanity—Faranza had carved a record in stone of his hideous crimes, of his mass murders and other atrocities, that he would leave behind to flaunt his invulnerability to countless generations. Even worse, future archeologists would ignore Faranza's insane confessions in stone and consider them only as the greatest examples of Olmec art ever discovered!

"You're a lunatic, Faranza," replied Deane. "Your mass sacrifices are as evil as the Nazi war crimes of World War II!"

The sculptor shook his bald head vigorously. "Yopi must be placated in order for spring to come each year. The blood of all Zoque must flow into the earth and Yopi's prophet must be reborn from the bodies of the dead!"

"But *you* claim to be Yopi, too!" Deane shouted. "*You're* responsible for these murders!"

"No, Steven," Faranza replied seriously. "They are not murders, but life-giving sacrifices which will allow the rest of Talzok to survive. And I am not Yopi until his spirit comes to me in the rituals at each crescent moon. Until then, I am his prophet, Luz."

Studying Faranza's hairless face, Deane realized that it was useless to talk to him. The sculptor had become totally insane—a paranoid, psychopathic killer with unlimited power to give full sway to his cruelest fantasies. And, like most psychopaths, he had retained enough contact with reality to protect himself against those who might try to destroy him.

Looking around, Deane saw the cavern was now filled with the deranged followers of Yopi-Luz, including both Zoque priests and Huastec warriors. Their heroic leader, Arras, was not there and Deane wondered if he was still alive.

"Tell me, Steven," said Faranza in Spanish, "what are the Children of Chan planning? They're a troublesome bunch of witches, I'll warn you, just in case that hag, Aruca, has cast her charms your way!"

Deane turned his head away from the insane Mayan, not wanting to say anything which might hurt Aruca and her cult's efforts to end Faranza's reign of terror.

"Ah! I see that she already has you in her spell!" Faranza exclaimed sadly. "Well, it doesn't matter. We will track her and her horde of witches to the edge of the world and end their treasonous heresy once and for all! But now, Steven, I wish to show those who doubt my power that Yopi-Luz is stronger even than the great Shutec. In my greatest triumph, I shall wear your flesh at the next lunar ritual!"

The mad sculptor shouted some commands to his retinue of servants and warriors in the chamber. Two Huastec spearmen grabbed Deane and dragged him from the cave. Within minutes, they were marching single-file in a torchlit procession which snaked along the rim of the mountain toward Talzok. Walking just behind Deane, Faranza was talking non-stop in Spanish about his humanitarian impact upon the region, as if it justified his mass atrocities.

The egomaniac was describing some of the public works projects he had begun in the primitive city, including drainage ditches, simple sanitation systems and—incredibly— ball fields! Faranza had taught the people a form of team handball he had invented, which sounded like a three-way mixture of lacrosse, soccer and war. He had even built a courtyard for the games, with inlaid serpentine tiles.

Remembering the fake serpentine tile Faranza had shown him in Merida such a long time before, Deane wished he had never agreed to let the shady counterfeiter of artifacts accompany him to the Olmec heartland!

The procession descended toward the floodplain of the future Rio Nefros with its endless fields of maize that fed the oppressed residents of Talzok. Walking in an absent-minded daze, Deane screened out the egocentric babbling of the deranged sculptor. They had just reached the first cornfield when the night air was suddenly filled with the horrible sounds of snarling beasts and screaming men!

Shadowy figures that were neither humans nor beasts pounced from the thick rows of maize where they had lain waiting for "Yopi" and his procession! Amid the confusion, Deane saw spotted jaguar fur covering the bodies of the ambushers. The Children of Chan had risen against the crazed butcher of Talzok!

"YOU did this to me, Shutec!" came Faranza's cry. "You and that witch, Aruca!"

Deane whirled around, throwing his body sideways just in time to avoid the Mayan's dagger thrust. It was difficult for Deane keep his balance in the moist corn field, especially with his wrists tied, and he dodged another rush by the insane "god" only to trip and crash to the wet ground.

Faranza's huge figure loomed over him, blotting out the night sky. Deane squirmed aside just as the sculptor buried the obsidian blade in the earth by his shoulder. Faranza raised the knife again, but this time his arm was seized by one of the sinister werecats before he could plunge it into Deane's chest.

Watching in horror, Deane saw other furry bodies swarm over Faranza, snarling and slashing at his hairless face and neck with inhuman fangs and claws. Faranza fell to the ground screaming as dark rivulets of blood appeared on his face and torso. Deane struggled to his feet just as two huge female jaguars pounced on the Mayan's writhing body to finish the gruesome vengeance begun by the half-human Children of Chan.

Then the werecats' golden eyes turned to Deane! Staggering to his feet, he started to run but was dragged down from behind.

Turn to page 201.

RETURN TO THE CAVE

Deane began to regret his decision to separate from Faranza. From what Aruca and the elder priestess had said, the key to their displacement in time lay in the Wall of Mists, not in Talzok or wherever the priests had led the sculptor.

"If Aruca has mastered the technique of time travel through the Mists, we can, too," he reasoned.

Deane resolved to wait for the Mayan inside the cave where they had parted company. He soon found the path that Aruca had taken a few minutes before, and within thirty or forty minutes he had returned to the mouth of the cave.

The scientist worked his way through the fissure into the passage and finally into the ritual chamber where the black basalt altar lay, its new blood still glistening in the rhythmic light of the Wall of Mists. While waiting for Faranza, he decided to use the time to study the mysterious Wall.

"The first thing to do is locate the source of that energy," he thought, staring at the ray of light leading to the pulsating red mass. "It might be just a projection, like a movie. Or perhaps it's some kind of monitoring system. Wherever the source is, I may find an intelligent being, whether from the 'stars' or not, keeping track of who comes in and out."

Deane tested his theory methodically. His first assumption was the simplest, namely that the Wall had to be a projection from above, much like the image on a movie screen being projected from a booth higher than the audience. Except for the bright flashes of light whenever something touched its surface, the Wall certainly seemed to be nothing more than an optical illusion.

Deane searched the floor of the cave until he had collected a handful of pebbles. Returning to the altar, he noted the angle of the Wall's surface (he estimated thirty degrees), which would determine the position of a conventional projector. Then he put his back to the lighted panel and tried to trace such a path toward the ceiling. In the deepest shadows, among a cluster of stalactites, he saw a pinpoint of white light, somewhat like a tiny unblinking star!

Deane kept his eyes on the dot and tossed a pebble over his shoulder at the translucent panel. Behind him, there was an instant flash as the small rock struck the massless gel. He saw a narrow, slanted pyramid of light flash upwards; its base at the Wall and the apex at the dot. Four faint rose-tinted lines even less tangible than strands of spider silk ran from the speck of light to the corners of the Wall.

"It's not the Wall that's being projected!" he realized. "Energy of some kind is being transmitted to the light in the cavern ceiling."

Deane waited until the usual clouds of mist had settled and the surface of the Wall was smooth. Then he tossed another pebble into the center of the nebulous barrier. Once more, he witnessed the small blast of white light which accompanied the production of the energy plane.

Turn to page 94.

THROUGH THE WALL

Deane didn't trust Trago. There were parts of his story which sounded factual enough, but others raised more questions than they answered. For example, who had been the other werejaguar at the monastery? How had Trago known about Deane's computer, or even recognized it, for that matter? According to his own story, he knew nothing about modern technology until a few years ago—hardly enough time to understand computer hardware. There was also the matter of his having been searching such a long time for his "sister;" why didn't he contact her as soon as he found her?

Deane felt confused. Some of Trago's story appeared to be true. His explanation of the details of the cavern and the mysterious teleportation of Faranza and him to the secret chamber was concise and logical.

Finally Deane made up his mind. The "Wall of Mists" held the key to the entire mystery, and he wanted to examine it alone.

"Go to your sister, Trago," Deane told the old hermit. "Find Aruca and protect her. Her 'disease' will never be understood. People will try to kill her no matter where she goes."

The old man's brown eyes watered, tears filling the deep wrinkles and furrows of his ancient face. "My gratitude is endless, scholar," he said, bowing formally from the waist with his perfect nineteenth century dignity and etiquette. "I call upon the saints of the conquistadores as well as my own gods to remember your courtesy. I pledge my word to you, scholar, that I shall return to guide you through the Wall to find your assistant and bring you both back to this time and place."

Trago rose and walked to the thick velvet curtain that hid the passage behind the bookshelf. Pausing, he turned to face Deane before leaving the entry chamber.

"Remain here in my dwelling where there is food and drink, my friend. Do not attempt to follow me. One's path through the mists can be diverted all too easily if things change in the present. Please do nothing which might interfere with the flow of energy within the Wall."

"I don't understand," Deane said, alarmed by this warning. "What do you mean about 'diverting one's path' inside the Wall?"

"There is no time for me to explain it to you, even if I understood it myself," Trago replied, with a hint of impatience in his voice. "Perhaps it is because there is so little difference between past and future. Anything that happens in one will seem much larger or more important in the other. It is as if the present exists only for the past or the future but never for itself. But let me go to Aruca. We will talk of such things when I return. Trust me, scholar, and remain in this room until I come back for you."

Turning away, Trago vanished into the tunnel that led to the ceremonial cavern. Waiting for the hermit's footsteps to die in the passage, Deane absently picked up the polished jade statue of the werejaguar and studied it. Its ferocious features and harsh anatomical realism became warmer and even beautiful in the glow of the soft lamp light.

But Deane's thoughts were not on the statue. Trago's partial explanation of the Wall's forces echoed in Deane's mind as he stroked the statue's delicately carved surface with his fingers. Deane was beginning to understand more of the old hermit's incredible story. Apparently the "Wall" was actually a kind of time boundary that responded to thought patterns! It could be used to travel through time, but only by intense concentration.

Deane suddenly lifted his head. He heard nothing. Trago was gone. Clutching the jade figurine, the scientist rose from the table and headed for the tunnel behind the bookshelves.

As soon as he entered the passage to the lower cavern, he saw the bright flash of light that meant Trago had just left the present. The Wall was opaque, its mysterious energy causing the internal masses of clouds to swirl furiously. Deane barely glimpsed the vanishing figure of the Zoque hermit. The dark outline of a tall man standing inside the Wall seemed to be receding into some nonexistent distance. He knew that the time boundary was only a few inches thick, but Trago's figure appeared to rushing outward, growing smaller as it vanished from the Wall.

Alone in the cavernous room, staring at the pulsating red wall, Deane hesitated. His entire world of physical sciences, so carefully studied and plotted, was crumbling. Did he dare go through with this? Did he believe in it?

He was suddenly aware of the Olmec sculpture in his hand, its cool smoothness and weight somehow reassuring amid all the weird circumstances he had encountered during the past few days. But as he looked down at it, the fanged jaws of the jade werejaguar glowed in the flashes of red light from the time barrier, appearing to grin evilly at the American. Its warmth was gone, its polished surface felt repulsive in Deane's hand.

Clutching the statuette, Deane stepped into the Wall. He concentrated intently on Luis Faranza's huge hands as he remembered them, carving delicate jade miniatures like Trago's werejaguar. The clouds within the Wall swirled thickly around him, blocking his view of the temple-cave. Once again, he felt the floating sensation but tried to ignore the lack of gravity. He intensified his concentration on the figurine until he could actually see Faranza's large hands holding the lump of jade that would become this sculpture.

The clouds within the Wall lightened around Deane almost at the same moment his feet began to feel solid ground. He continued to concentrate on the jade figurine, unwilling to risk being trapped in an alien time period. It was the sound of many frightened human voices that caused him to raise his head.

He was in the temple chamber once more but he was no longer alone. Through the translucent film of the Wall, he could see a throng of warriors brandishing long spears with tips of black volcanic glass. Instead of the rounded helmets he remembered from his first view of the cavern, they wore caps of jaguar hide decorated with the multicolored plumages of innumerable varieties of tropical birds.

A huge man, naked to the waist and wearing a hideously carved wooden mask, stood in front of the stone altar, holding a small jade axe in one hand and an obsidian dagger in the other. A slender woman dressed in a loose white garment lay stretched across the gory stone. Her arms and legs were being held by two men wearing smaller versions of the mask covering the giant's face. Deane could see only that she was a beautiful Indian girl, perhaps in her early twenties, and that she was unconscious.

"Hear your servant, Terrible One!" the huge masked man was praying, his weapons raised high above the altar. "Luz calls to you, Great Yopi. Take this offering of life energy and use it to create new life! Know that this witch before you is the changeling hag, Aruca, priestess of the Children of Chan, who has offended your people with her disobedience and sacrilege."

It took a few seconds for the words of the prayer and the scene to penetrate Deane's confused mind. The giant priest was going to sacrifice a girl named Aruca! The slender obsidian blade had already started to descend when the scientist leapt through the Wall behind the large cleric and grabbed his powerful arm.

The warriors, seeing Deane's golden-bearded figure come leaping through the Wall and grab their priest, began to shout in terror.

"There! In the Wall!"

"It is Shutec himself!"

"Look, the Lord Shutec is attacking the Prophet Luz!"

The huge man was as strong as a horse, but the surprise of Deane's sudden assault allowed the scientist enough time to push him away from the altar. Deane whirled around and lifted the unconscious body of the Indian woman in his arms, glaring fiercely at her two awe-stricken guards, who hurriedly backed away.

"Put that witch down, Steven Deane!"

Faranza! The sculptor's muffled voice speaking in English from behind the wooden mask startled Deane. Amazed, he could merely stand, dumbfounded, with his back against the black altar and the woman in his arms.

The giant priest removed the mask, and now Deane saw that the Mayan had shaved all the hair from his head and face, even his eyebrows, and coated his skin with some kind of clear grease. He seemed to have aged years as well!

"What's going on, Luis?" Deane cried. "You were going to murder this woman!"

"My name is no longer 'Luis,' " said Faranza sternly. "Here I am known as 'Luz,' the Prophet of Yopi. The vile creature you hold in your arms is the terrible witch, Aruca. You yourself witnessed her change into a wild beast near Monte Azul!"

Deane glanced down at the girl's still features. Her thick black hair fell in sensuous waves across her smooth, tanned forehead. It seemed impossible even to imagine that she was the withered and wrinkled woman at the ruins!

"I don't believe you, Luis, or 'Luz,' " Deane replied, just as the woman began to stir. "But even if I did, I'd stop you from killing her!"

"You fool! Don't meddle in things you don't understand. This woman is the leader of a cult of werejaguars, the Children of Chan. They have terrorized everyone in the ancient city of Talzok! I have sworn to kill them all— every man, woman, child, and infant!"

"You're crazy!" Deane yelled. The warriors in the chamber had been silent, but now—hearing a stranger they thought was a god challenge their holy Prophet in unknown foreign words—they became confused and started mumbling among themselves. Faranza called to them in their own language.

"The great Lord Shutec has returned, as I promised. But he is unwell. He has entered a diseased human body. He must be freed of it the way that we free the souls of the Children of Chan from their changeling bodies. I, Luz, Prophet of Yopi, will wear his flesh at the next moon rite!"

Deane was so astonished by Faranza's words that he failed to notice the Indian woman regain consciousness. She raised her head in time to hear the Prophet's words. Twisting out of Deane's grasp, she jumped to the floor of the chamber and ran for the Wall.

"Stop her!" screamed Faranza. A shower of spears struck the clouded surface only moments after Aruca's lithe shape had vanished. Deane's last glimpse of the beautiful woman was unsettling. She was sneering at *him* with an expression of such hatred that he was numb to the rough hands that seized him!

Turn to page 159.

Turn to page 159.

THE STARMEN

Deane grabbed the hermit's fragile arm. The muscles were flabby and withered beneath the white cotton sleeve, and Deane feared that he would crush the birdlike bones with his sudden grip. He relaxed the pressure, but not enough to let Trago go free as he pulled the hermit closer to the table.

"I don't trust you, Trago. Even if you're telling the truth about coming back, something could happen to you on the other side of the Wall. Help me find my assistant and my equipment now! It shouldn't take you very long, since you know the Mists so well. Then you can pick up your sister's trail. Surely a few more hours can't matter that much."

Trago's wrinkled face was carefully expressionless in the soft lamp light. Finally he nodded. "As you wish, scholar," he said coldly. "Release my arm and follow me to the Wall."

Deane followed the shaman behind the bookshelf and through the fissure which led to the inner passage. As they emerged into the brightly lit ritual chamber, Trago pointed to the pulsating panel of light at its far end.

"When we enter the Wall, keep your hand on my arm and let your mind empty itself of all thoughts except the feel of my flesh beneath the cloth," he instructed Deane.

Trago trotted past the intricately sculpted columns of limestone with Deane at his heels. They skirted the altar and went directly to the transparent red rectangle with its pyramidal beam extending upward to the deeper shadows of the cavern's ceiling. The scientist stared for a moment at the tiny point of brilliant light where the sides of the pyramid converged and then reached for Trago's skeletal arm.

The Zoque hermit approached the Wall and stepped into the shimmering red mists with Deane clutching his sleeve. As before, a sudden flare momentarily blinded him as the two entered the dimensional gate, but he was expecting it this time and managed to concentrate only on Trago's arm. Instead of the dazzling array of blurred images and roughness underfoot, Deane was conscious only of a drifting, floating sensation as they seemed to move without direction through the billowing red and black clouds.

Suddenly, the image of Faranza's figure leaped into Deane's mind. The huge Mayan seemed to be running through a thick forest—no, a swamp! He was splashing through stagnant pools of water and mud, dodging the countless vines and creepers hanging from heavy limbs of swamp trees. In that brief flash of clairvoyance, Deane saw Faranza's sweaty face contorted with a look of horror and fear. At least he thought it was Faranza's face! The sculptor had shaved all the hair off his face and head. For an instant, Deane completely lost his concentration on Trago's arm.

All at once, the clouds within the Wall darkened and he thought he heard Trago's voice yelling. "Your hand! Think of your hand!"

Beneath Deane, the ground solidified instantly, causing him to stumble and drag his feet painfully across hard rock. Deane realized suddenly that the sensation of being dragged was different this time. Before, when Trago was taking him to the present, it seemed that he was being dragged forward, his toes stumbling as if he were rushing uncontrollably down a steep embankment and could not keep his balance.

Now it seemed that he was being hurled away from Trago. There was a sensation of something ripping their minds as well as their flesh apart.

"You lied to me!" Deane screamed amid the fury of the Wall around him. "You're taking me into the future!" He jerked his arm, trying to free himself from Trago's grasp.

But there was no answer. The grip on his arm was strong, stronger than that old man's grip could be!

Something grabbed Deane's wrist, closing around it like steel bands on his arm. Suddenly Deane was moving again, being pulled against his will into the clouds of the Wall. He reached out with his left hand to tear the fingers away, but another hand snared his free wrist as well.

Deane jerked his body, trying to wrestle himself loose, but it was impossible to gain any leverage while he was floating. Every move he made seemed to magnify his captor's strength and work against him. Suddenly he realized why he could not break free. The struggle itself was focusing his thoughts upon the hands! It was having just the opposite effect of transporting him wherever his captor willed them to go!

"I've got to fight with my own will!" Deane realized.

He stopped struggling against the supernatural forces being used to take him into the future, focusing instead upon Faranza's face as he had glimpsed the Mayan giant only moments earlier. Almost immediately, the image filled his mind. Faranza's sweat-streaked, hairless face became the center of a vortex, a tornado of red and black clouds which funneled into the dense swamp. The sculptor was running for his life!

His captor's hand tore at Deane's flesh, tearing his thoughts away from Faranza. The vortex dimmed and he almost lost the tiny image at the distant end of the funnel. Forcing himself to ignore the painful grasp, Deane concentrated on his friend's running figure. The more Deane was able to block out the presence of his captor, the closer he seemed to come to Faranza. The large Mayan was so near

---

in the linguist's mind that he could almost feel the humid air of the swamp and smell the decaying matter in the black water that reached to his friend's waist.

"Luis!" he called impulsively. The Mayan jerked his hairless head around as if he had heard Deane's voice but could not place it in space. His eyes had a wild, hunted look Deane had never seen before on his robust face.

"Here, Luis! I'm here!" Deane shouted. It seemed as if he could reach out his hand and touch his friend on the shoulder, but it was only an illusion of the Wall, like the distorted nearness of the moon's craters through a powerful telescope.

In another corner of his mind, Deane heard distant laughter. As soon as the new sound impinged upon his disturbing vision of Faranza, Deane felt himself being pulled away from the narrow end of the swirling vortex.

"It requires the discipline of centuries to bend the forces of the Wall, young scholar."

The voice appeared in his tired mind without warning. Each word was louder and clearer than the last, sweeping the thoughts of Faranza's flight through the swamp from Deane's brain just as his assistant's body was overtaken by a formless mass of yellow and black fur.

As his mental view of the swamp telescoped away from the struggling Faranza and the nameless horror attacking him, Deane became aware once more of the steely grip of his captor's fingers digging into the flesh of his wrists. Deane made a final desperate attempt to regain control of his direction within the Wall, but his captor's will was much too powerful. Deane felt the energy flowing from him, seeming to drain away into the swirling mists of the Wall. . . .

Strange hissing noises were the next sounds Deane

heard. He was unable to move a muscle, not even an eyelid, but his mind was either conscious or dreaming. He saw or imagined himself inside a transparent capsule, surrounded by sterile white walls and gleaming silver metal. The hissing was coming from a machine filling the capsule with a colorless, odorless fog.

Alien thoughts lurked on the fringes of his mind like the conversation of doctors and nurses in a recovery room following surgery. The hissing sounds incorporated themselves into a nightmarish dream of reptilian creatures with slick scaly heads, who—it seemed—were discussing him in their sibilant language.

"Did you remove the vessel from the field?" one of them asked.

"Yes, but not before the old human dived back into it. He had constructed a field monitor. We must leave this sector at once."

"What of this one?" asked a third reptile. "His brain is becoming more active."

"Use the temporal bender," the second voice ordered. "Enter the last origin coordinates of the field generator. Early sixty-eighth millenium, I believe."

"The humans of that sector are close to a primitive unification, Neenas," objected the first. "Is it safe to release him with his knowledge of the field?"

"They are also fascinated with insanity, I believe," said the third.

"Kran is right," agreed the being called Neenas. "In fact, he is understating the case. Humans of that period seem almost obsessed with mental disease. We know that true unification will not be applied prior to the seventieth millenium. Most intelligentsia of his sector will consider his report to be either fantasy or madness."

In Deane's nightmare, he tried to rise from the cushioned surface where he lay but could not move a muscle. His eyes were open and he could see the shining brown head of the creature named Kran as he leaned over the linguist's immobile body. It was not the head of a reptile, but the completely bald head of a large human with beige skin and almond-shaped eyes.

"Is he awake, Kran?" asked the one in charge.

"Yes, Neenas. He is listening to us." The being's lips had not moved. Deane was "listening" only with his mind.

"Use a monitor. Scan him," the commander ordered tersely.

As the being named Kran held a blue nonmetallic cube inches away from Deane's forehead, he tried again to will his helpless muscles to move but they would not respond. Then Deane remembered the story Trago had told him about the aliens who taught the Children of Chan how to change their forms. Trago had been specific about a "blue cube" they had used to communicate with his primitive kinspeople.

"He knows of the visitation in sector thirty-one," reported Kran. "He is a scientist who witnessed a transformation by one of the subjects in the mortality experiment—a woman named Aruca."

"What kind of scientist?" demanded the unnamed third alien.

"Not a physical scientist," answered Kran. "A linguist. Humans of the sixty-eighth continue to speak different languages. This one specializes in the dialects spoken over a three-millenium range in a small area surrounding field location eight."

"Mayan?" asked his companion.

"That, along with Zoque, Huastec, and Spanish."

"How did he find the Field?" asked the commander. "It

is known to so few humans in that sector."

"He did not find it," the subordinate reported. "He accidentally recorded the woman's will-words just as she was transforming to enter the Field. She took the form of a wild feline, a jaguar, just as he approached and he was driven by curiosity to understand what he had witnessed."

"How did he reach the vessel?" asked the nameless one.

"It was happenstance, an infinitesimal improbability," Kran replied. "The will-words were mixed randomly in the memory of an archaic Thinker. The old man had redesigned the Thinker's circuits to emulate one of our monitors and homed on the transmitter vessel in Sector Thirty-One. He even constructed a secret work room behind the transmitter to protect himself from the superstitious primitives around him. It seems that the elder who programmed the Thinker with the will-words is now lost in time."

"How incredible!" said the commander. "Have they managed to avoid critical displacements?"

"This one has, but we can't be sure about his lost companion. But then, I doubt if anything more than the usual aesthetic or philosophical shifts in cycle would result from such a minor displacement event."

"Does he know how to transmit?"

"Very clumsily, although the old one who brought him into the vessel seems to have enough knowledge to build a monitor," answered Kran. "It is not clear why the other man came except that he sought the contactee, Aruca. This one seems to have been heading back for something, until we took control."

"Preunification humans are very frail, Anagil," explained the commander to the silent alien. "They are capable of Class Four mentation if properly taught, yet they allow themselves to be manipulated by others rather easily. That is how we have managed to engineer their sense of time in such a simplistic manner. It is as far as two thousand years from this man's home sector to the time when they will begin to understand the real relationship between time and space. Scientists of his sector still refer to it as a 'spacetime continuum.' "

The unseen creature called "Anagil" made a clucking noise which sounded only inches away from Deane's immobile head. "How could he believe that past, present and future are separate after his experience in the Field?" asked the novice.

"Perhaps he does not," suggested Kran, shifting the blue cube minutely across Deane's scalp, "but that is what Neena is saying. Even if he tries to communicate his first-hand experiences to his fellow scientists, they will not believe him because time is viewed so differently in that sector."

"I think we will be safe from detection if we simply return him to his last entry point and bend the Field away from his sector," added Neena. "There may be some minor adjustments here and there as a result of the older man's temporal displacements, but certainly no more than we encountered in the immortality reversal experiment."

"That's probably already happened anyway," Kran agreed. "The old one must have introduced thousands of alterations if he has been collecting all the necessary components for a field monitor. I suspect that he has created something of a mystery for his dupes."

"Such alterations will be minor, I assure you," soothed Neena. "I have witnessed temporal displacements many times before and I know how coincidental such irregularities usually are. A new lineage here, an unexplained culture there, none of it matters very long outside its original sector, you know."

"Shall we bend the Field, then?" asked Kran.

"I think so," replied his commander. "This man's scientific curiosity as well as his personal interests would lead him back to it no matter how carefully we erased the memory. Send him back, Kran."

The being leaning over Deane's frozen body pressed a control button or lever of some kind. The perfectly contoured capsule rose soundlessly toward the lighted ceiling. Deane saw three long bars emerge from the domed walls and track across the rotunda toward himself. As they neared his position, he could see that they were the disjointed sides of some kind of pyramidal chamber which would float suspended in the very center of the rotunda. He would be lying on the square base of a pyramid hovering off the floor of this strange chamber while the sides which now floated toward him would form its four triangular walls.

Without a sound, the four sides and the base of the pyramid locked together perfectly. Still immobile, Deane expected total darkness to descend upon him when the walls were in place, but they were made of some glassine material which was translucent enough to fill the interior with soft filtered light. Deane felt the sensation of being lifted outside of the capsule. His body rose without supports until it lay suspended in mid-air at the center of the pyramid. Then the shape began to turn, very slowly at first, around his inert form.

He watched the four seams at the apex of the pyramid, where the triangular sides were joined. They were spinning around above his motionless eyes, the only sign of movement in his tomb-like cage. The visual impact was hypnotic. He tried to turn away from the steady flicker of the lines but was unable to move even his eyeballs. He felt his mind slipping away from his control. . . .

It was dark. Opening his eyes, Deane found himself lying on a hard stone floor in the thickest blackness he had ever experienced. Both the Wall and the aliens' pyramid had disappeared completely. Groping in his pocket, Deane felt the reassuring bulge of the Bic lighter. He brought the lighter out of his pocket without sitting up, not knowing how high the ceiling might be above his head. The flare of the butane flame was blinding, but it revealed what he suspected. He was in the temple-cave, just as it had appeared when Trago had brought him through the Wall. Deane stood up.

Turn to page 181.

LOST!

The lighter's tiny flame flickered across the scores of stalagmites and columns carved into stelae. Deane was standing behind the massive altar with its ancient bloodstains and carved figures on its sides. But it was dark . . . too dark. . . .

The red Wall! It was gone!

Quickly Deane looked over to where the Wall of Mists had been. He groped forward with one hand, expecting to see the flash of red light which would signal his contact with the Wall of Mists. But it did not happen. The Wall was gone or had it ever existed?

Turning away, Deane made his way among the many stelae on the cavern floor, looking for the narrow passage which he and Trago had used to reach the hermit's quarters. The Bic grew overheated and began to burn his thumb where he was holding the fuel switch. Just as he released the valve to let the lighter cool, he spotted an irregular niche in the cavern wall several dozen yards away. Then the lighter flicked out.

Deane forced himself to wait, although he was impatient to reach Trago's chamber. He was beginning to wonder if it had all been a dream. Finding Trago's quarters would prove to himself that these strange events had been real. As soon as the lighter cooled off, Deane flicked it on and, by its light, plunged forward through the niche.

The passage was just as he remembered it, both from his explorations with Faranza and from his encounter with Trago. Once inside the twisting tunnel, he extinguished the flame and felt his way forward with his hands on the cramped walls. Just as before, the blackness was absolute; it was such a dense darkness that he could not see his hands before his face. He was trying to judge his distance when his feet struck some kind of light object on the cavern floor. The sudden clatter alarmed him. Putting his hand down, he felt something large and heavy blocking the corridor in front of him. He struck the lighter, then stifled an involuntary cry.

It was a mummified body, clad in a tarnished metal breastplate! He had kicked the visored helmet away from the mummy's skull that now focused its eyeless sockets on the dazzling flame of the Bic lighter. Terrified, Deane dropped the lighter, plunging himself and the tunnel into total darkness. He heard the lighter strike against the metal armor of the mummy.

There was a light rustling sound from the floor near the mummy. Something ran against the ankle nearest the corpse's side. At the same time, a loud crash of metal against stone caused him to back away in horror!

Then he heard squeals. Cave rats! Deane sighed in relief. Yelling a quick "Hey!" he kicked the side of the mummy. The tunnel was filled with shrill cries and the scampering noises of rodent feet on the rock floor. When silence returned to the passage, Deane squatted and crawled forward until he touched the hard dried skin of the mummy's face. His hand recoiled at the gruesome touch, but he gritted his teeth and continued to search the ancient corpse for the fallen lighter.

He found it nestled among the rotten cloth of the pantaloons which barely draped the skeleton's leg bones. His hand was shaking so badly that it took him several attempts to light the lighter. Its bright flame reflected dimly from the tarnished metal of the breastplate that was now hollow, its contents gnawed to nothing by countless generations of rats, whose descendants now used the armored chest cavity as a nest.

———

Deane glanced to the opposite side of the mummified skeleton and saw what had crashed to the floor only moments before. A torch! Made of resinous wood, it was fitted into a brass holder. This unknown conquistador must have fallen on the firebrand only moments before he died, Deane speculated.

Retrieving the torch, Deane ignited its end easily, the highly volatile resin flaring into a bright, smoky flame.

Standing up, Deane stared down at the skeletal warrior. The breastplate looked authentic, as did the fabric of the pantaloons and the Spanish leather of the conquistador's boots. He had seen collections of such armor and clothing in several different museums and was positive that these were original sixteenth century materials. What puzzled him was the fact that he had not seen the corpse earlier, when Trago ushered him along this very passageway!

That recalled his original purpose to mind. Stepping over the skeleton, Deane hurried toward the entry chamber which the Zoque hermit used as a home. The narrow opening was still there, but was no longer hidden by the shelves on the opposite side. Deane felt his heart sinking. Hurriedly he squeezed into the chamber, then stopped.

It was empty. Even the fireplace was gone. Although the fissure was in the same place, there was no sign of there ever having been a fire in that spot! There was no sign that anyone had ever been here at any time!

Deane stared around in horror and disbelief, trying to determine whether he had dreamed the entire episode. He began to rummage in every corner of the room for evidence of the old hermit's existence but found nothing. He even located the outer entrance to the cavern, which was exactly where he remembered it to be, but discovered that it was overgrown with brambles and mountain shrubs so thick that it was invisible from the lower slopes. Some of the bramble bushes were so old that they were as thick as his leg.

It was obviously an ancient cave, perhaps undisturbed since a lone Spaniard had entered it several centuries before. There were some late Mayan paintings, and perhaps even some Aztecan designs, on the wall where Trago's bookshelves had been. Deane recognized the glyphs of warning and death spaced around the narrow opening to the temple-chamber with its Olmec altar and stelae.

"They knew about the Wall, too," Deane muttered to himself, "and they declared it a tabooed place. No wonder it has remained empty for so long—except for Trago!"

The mystery was even greater because he had stumbled over the mummy going out, but not going in to the inner chamber from this one. He was almost ready to believe that Trago had returned and somehow managed to remove all the evidence of his presence! The old hermit might have even placed the mummy in the passageway to mislead—

Deane halted his wild theorizing as the simplest explanation of all occurred to him. If he accepted the reality of the Wall in the first place, then it was easy to imagine that Trago had merely taken him to the cavern before the conquistador had fallen across the passage. It was just that simple! And then something had happened to Trago, something that resulted in his complete disappearance along with everything associated with him!

Trago's total existence seemed to have been erased from the earth. "Yet everything is exactly the same as it was when Trago and I arrived," Deane thought. "The stelae and the altar are still there even if the Wall . . ."

Deane broke off his confused thoughts and raced for the narrow entrance to the inner tunnel. He squeezed himself inside the passage, his torch burning brightly in the pitch-black corridor. The linguist ran along the tunnel, bounding over the armored mummy without pausing, and continued running until he reached the cathedral chamber with the stelae and altar. He hurriedly checked a few of the stelae he had studied and determined that they were the same. Then he turned to the rear of the chamber beyond the huge bloodstained altar.

Stepping closer to the rear wall of the cavern, he was barely able to make out the outline of a heavy slab which seemed to protrude from the back wall—the secret entrance he and Faranza had discovered.

Deane scrambled forward and pushed his entire weight against the massive boulder. At first it seemed to be part of the unyielding wall. Turning, he put his back against the slab and bent his knees for additional leverage. The long-unused portal began to slide away from the narrow tunnel, flooding the already stale air of the cavern with a musty stench like the one he had smelled near the mummy.

"Damn rats are everywhere!" he cursed, as he peered into the passage by the light of his torch and saw what he hoped to find on the floor just inside the secret door.

The ancient clay lamp was just as he had left it, although the wick with its animal fat had been eaten by rats. He nudged the small pot to one side with his foot and stepped forward, his heart pounding wildly. Soon he would know whether he had imagined the adventures of the past few days or if they were real! He burst into the secret inner chamber, sending a horde of squealing cave rats scurrying to the hundreds of crevices and crannies beside the wall to hide from the torchlight.

Deane's feet kicked huge clouds of powdery dust into the smoky light of the firebrand, giving the chamber an eerie murkiness. Squinting, he tried to peer through the suffocating fog of centuries-old dust to find the proof he needed of his own sanity. It no longer mattered if he could convince others of what had happened in this remote cavern. He needed desperately to know for himself how much of it had been real.

And there it was, barely visible through the thick layers of white limestone dust which covered everything in this small secret chamber! The camp table had disintegrated into gnawed splinters eons ago. The portable computer lay broken on the stone floor where it had crashed as the table collapsed unknown centuries earlier. The plastic casing had been gnawed by countless generations of rats, as had the bulky marine battery under the debris of the table. The skeletons of several rodents lay scattered around the junk, perhaps poisoned by the battery acid which had leaked away through the gnawed blue cube.

Deane stepped closer and nudged the computer with his foot. A frantic squealing erupted as a litter of baby rats poured from the console and scurried for the deeper shadows near the wall. Nodding grimly, he shoved the machine aside. Then he went immediately to the cairn of rocks where he had hidden the diskette with its recording of Aruca's chant.

As Deane cast aside the fragments of the disintegrated diskette and nudged the cracked, brittle power cable with his foot, he wondered about Faranza. His Mayan assistant was trapped in the past, among the people who would someday carve the very artifacts he had copied and sold to tourists in Merida. Angry tears welled in his eyes as Deane recalled the last mental image he'd had of the burly sculptor, running through some ancient swamp, being mauled by fearful two-legged creatures wearing the beautiful spotted pelts of jaguars.

Wiping his eyes, Deane stared at the debris at his feet. Then he kicked the small computer aside as he ducked into the passage leading away from the secret room. When he reached the cavern with its incredible collection of Olmec sculpture, he sealed Trago's hidden workroom with the same rock panel that had guarded it from everything except rats for the past thirty centuries.

Turn to page 213.

FARANZA'S SIGNATURE

Deane nodded toward the bookshelf that hid the passage to the ritual cavern.

"Go to your sister, Trago," Deane told the hermit, "but try to hurry. If what you're telling me is true about the Huastec's ruthlessness, I want to get Faranza and the computer out of there as soon as possible."

The dignified Trago bowed. "You are indeed an honorable man, scholar," he said. "Be assured that I shall never forget your trust and your compassion. Remain here. Do not attempt to travel alone through the Wall because it will endanger both of us. I shall return as quickly as possible to take you to your assistant."

"All right! All right! I believe you," Deane said impatiently. "Now go on and take care of your sister before it's too late to help either one of them!"

Trago left the table and disappeared behind the shelf. Deane waited until he was sure that the hermit was inside the inner passage, then he squeezed his slim body through the fissure and followed after the old man.

At the tunnel's exit into the well-lighted ceremonial chamber, he paused to watch Trago enter the Wall of Mists. The Zoque hermit walked around the altar and stepped into the Wall. The flare of energy blinded Deane for a moment. When he could see again, the black-fringed red clouds were swirling furiously around Trago's tall figure. Each time the masses of clouds rolled across the shaman, his outline became less distinct. He appeared to dissolve so gradually that Deane could not tell exactly when he vanished.

"Well, good luck!" Deane murmured, watching the seething clouds settle into the transparent rose mist of the mysterious Wall. Then he turned his gaze away from the altar and toward scores of columns scattered throughout the inner cavern. The excellent Olmec stelae gleamed in the bright torchlight, accented by the soft flashes of pink light from the Wall of Mists. Their sculpted surfaces were perfectly distinct, as if they had been freshly cut into the stalagmites. From his view facing the ancient bloodstained altar, they seemed to be tombstones, lending a sombre graveyard atmosphere to the ritual chamber.

Deane remembered the first view he and Faranza had of this same chamber, when the flat-topped boulder was uncarved and the original stalagmites protruded from the cave floor in the red light of the Wall, like blood stained teeth inside the mouth of some huge monster.

"Assuming that this is the same place, these stelae had to be carved between then and now," Deane reasoned. "If just one man, Trago perhaps, had done it, the job would take forever! But, then again, how long has he been living in these unexplored mountains? Hermits have been known to do incredible artistic work during their isolated lifetimes."

This new idea was interesting. If Deane could demonstrate that the old man had done all of these sculptures himself, a slender thread would exist to connect Deane's previous world of cause and effect, of obedient laws of time and space, to this one of temporal chaos. The notion blossomed instantly into an obsession. Deane was determined to prove that Trago had produced these replicas of Olmec work himself.

In his mounting excitement, Deane darted back into the corridor leading to the Zoque's quarters. "Trago's stone-cutting tools must be hidden somewhere in that chamber!" he thought. "An expert can match the cuts and gouges on these rocks and artifacts with the slight imperfections on blades and chisels!"

Deane squeezed once more through the slit that opened into the chamber behind the tall bookshelf. The hermit's cot of dried grasses was the first place he looked. Stripping the well-made peasant bed, he hoped to discover a cache of tools somewhere beneath it. The rabbit skins were perfectly cured and sewn together into one of the finest blankets Deane had ever seen, and the cotton cloth sheets were made of flour sack material that had been washed so often they were as light and soft as tissue paper. The mattress was nothing more than a simple pallet of dried grasses, carefully chosen for the hermit's comfort. It was obvious that Trago was a meticulous man, who planned his comforts well and spent the necessary time to insure them. But there were no tools of any kind hidden among the covers of the bed.

Deane turned to the shaman's pantry—nothing more than a pile of dried food and utensils in one corner of the chamber. The old man's provisions were meager but adequate. He had small stores of dried beans, corn, meal, peppers, and some kind of wild green vegetable with very broad leaves, even when dried. Deane's search of each sack was thorough, but revealed nothing that might prove Trago's hand had been the hand that carved the stelae in the ritual chamber.

With the same methodical attention, Deane went through the rest of the chamber, but found no signs of tools. In fact, the only bladed implement he discovered was a table knife on the mantel which had been sharpened so many times that it was almost as thin as foil. He even leaned inside the natural fissure that served as a chimney, but found nothing but a thick layer of soot.

Each time he passed by the table, the jade werejaguar statuette appeared to be grinning even more maliciously, as if it were enjoying his frustration. Finally, Deane turned to the bookshelf, hoping that Trago might have sketched one of his carvings before sculpting it.

Several dozen volumes stood there, collectors' editions of eighteenth and nineteenth century leather-bound books, all written in the stilted academic Spanish of that era. There were dictionaries, medical encyclopedias, technical reference works on botany, chemistry, and physics, and even some rare editions of prominent philosophical studies of the period. Deane marveled at the range of Trago's interests, and decided that the old hermit's story about the mission education might have had some truth in it.

Thumbing through one of the physics manuals, a tissue drawing slipped from between its pages and wafted to the rock floor. Hoping it was a drawing of a sculpture, Deane picked it up. He gasped in astonishment. It appeared to be a modern circuit design for some kind of an electronic apparatus! Lacking the technical training to read the schematic drawing, Deane tried to guess at its nature.

The clear black lines had been drawn with such precision that he could trace any one of the thousands of paths with his naked eye. It resembled a schematic for a radio or television set, but had ten times the usual number of connections. Deane was ready to admit defeat when he noticed where the diagram had been stuffed in the old physics book.

It was next to an antique drawing of a curious machine that seemed to be a cross between an abacus and a steam calliope. Deane recognized it immediately. It was Charles Babbage's "cyphering" device, the first design of a digital computer! Babbage had never been able to make it work because he lacked the proper engineering tools and money. Still, its operating principle was sound and it was designed to do the same work that modern computers do, but with steam, pistons and gears rather than electricity and silicon chips.

Deane suddenly recalled Trago's mention of a "cyphering machine" and realized that he must have taken the term from this nineteenth century book. The thin paper schematic in his hand was much more recent, but it was a design for a computer, too. Deane had seen logic circuits before, but he had never seen one as complicated as this one. In fact, it almost seemed to be years, perhaps even decades, ahead of its time.

"So Trago was lying about not knowing anything about computers!" Deane thought with a chill. "And probably about many other things as well!"

Frantically, he pulled every book and pamphlet from the shelves, leafing through each one carefully, but found nothing else to give him any more clues about the old hermit.

"This is staged!" Deane thought with a flash of insight. "Everything is *exactly* the way Trago wants it to appear to outsiders, except for that schematic! It's a fresh drawing, and I'll bet anything I own that he overlooked it when he set up this scene."

Then Deane stopped in frustration. Even if the drawing demonstrated Trago's understanding of computer design, it did not explain how the hermit had tampered with the game program. Nor did it suggest how Trago had carved the Olmec stelae of the ritual chamber in such a short time.

Irritably returning the books to their shelves, Deane sat down at the table, staring at the jade figurine before him. It was virtually identical to the ones he had seen among Faranza's many excellent forgeries. He had studied them hundreds of times, and had even sketched a few of them. It was Faranza's attention to detail that made the fake Olmec pieces beautiful. That same attention was visible in this

statue. Whoever made it had carved such a perfect counterfeit example of Olmec style that it too would be unde-
tectable by practically any expert analysis. Its only flaw
was the lack of scars, scratches, and stains one would
expect on an archeological artifact.

Deane reached for the werejaguar figurine to examine
its etched lines in closer detail. He wanted to be absolutely
certain that it was free of grave dirt and the red clay which
covered and stained everything buried longer than a few
days in the Monte Azul area.

The fine details were more accurate than he remembered. He counted the inner rows of human teeth and
found them to be exactly correct. The outer teeth of the
jaguar were spaced differently, as they would be in the jaws
of a feline carnivore. Even the eyes were perfect, with a
thin line representing the nictitating membrane of the jungle cat.

Deane shifted his position to take advantage of the
torchlight and continued his examination of the figurine.
The details of the human viscera were very precise, as if
they had been sculpted by someone with a surgeon's
knowledge of anatomy. The linguist glanced at the old
medical encyclopedias on the shelves and smiled. Then he
saw the mark. It was almost invisible, wedged between the
two stomachs of the werejaguar.

"My God!" he muttered, reaching for the lamp with its
sooty base. Hurriedly he wiped the inside of the hot chimney with his finger, coating it with feathery lampblack.
Then he rubbed the mark he had just found, making its
finely incised lines stand out starkly against the pale green
jade. It was a microscopic but very clear equal sign with a
tiny circle above it—Faranza's signature mark!

With shaking hands, Deane turned the polished statuette so that the flickering lantern light could illuminate its

every contour. The Mayan sculptor's style was everywhere, in every line and curve of the piece. Deane swore silently at himself for not having noticed it earlier. He rotated the miniature sculpture completely and was staring once more at the grinning double muzzle which was a mixture of a jaguar and a death's head when its outline wavered.

It happened just as the lamplight dimmed, and Deane thought for a moment that the unsteady light had tricked his eyes. But then it happened again and he was positive of the change in both the appearance and the feel of the figurine. For only an instant, the features of the werejaguar softened. The deeply incised outlines had faded, becoming so weakly defined that he could hardly see them. At exactly the same moment, the lamp dimmed again, the room darkened, and he felt the weight of the jade statue lighten in his hand, as if someone had removed it from his palm!

Deane clenched the Olmec figure, as if he were protecting it from some unseen spectral thief, but he was too late. The object's mass and weight vanished from his closed fist just as the chamber was plunged into blackness. The sturdy wooden bench disappeared from beneath him, sending him crashing painfully to the stone floor. When he recovered from the shock of his fall, he realized that the only light in the room was coming from the outer entry passage.

In the murky half-light, he could see that his surroundings were very different. The table and bench had vanished, along with Trago's cot and bookshelf! Shaking the stupor from his head, Deane struggled to his feet. As he stood in the darkened cavern, he stirred a thick layer of fine dust on the floor, causing it to billow around him in a suffocating cloud. He stumbled, sneezing and coughing, toward the dimly lit entrance. The dust grew thicker. He coughed so he could barely stand.

Deane made his way to the entrance of the hermit's cave, only to find it overgrown with briar and laurel bushes so old that some of the main stems were more than a foot in diameter! The entire mouth of Trago's home was covered so well by the thick mountain shrubs that it was completely hidden from the trail that wound along the slope toward Monte Azul in the valley below him.

Deane's eyes glazed in confusion and fear as he tried to apply reason and logic to what had just happened. His memory was a jumble of obscure Zoque phrases, Olmec designs, werejaguars, and a red haze that covered it all. Luis Faranza's broad face suddenly dominated the bewildering collage of visions. Deane shook his head, trying to stifle the disturbing images, but they remained in his brain.

Feeling light-headed and confused, Deane began to climb down the steep mountain slope to the trail below. His mind seemed empty—drained of both energy and intelligence—as he stumbled and slid through the rough brush and brambles to the rugged trace.

The old postman whose daily route from Monte Azul to Kaktunque led him along the same mountain trail recognized the young American's face, though it was scarred and bleeding from a fall. But it was obvious that the dazed young man did not recognize him. The postman helped the young man settle himself securely on the burro's back, like one of the packages tied there, then started on his long trip to the village of Kaktunque.

Turn to page 213.

THE CANTINA

"Wait a mintue!" exclaimed Deane. "I don't know what you did or how you did it, but this is the craziest thing I've ever heard of! Did you drug me in that cantina? That's it, isn't it? You drugged me and somehow led me out of the bar while Luis was occupied with those women."

Order had suddenly returned to the scientist's world. Deane had forgotten that the simplest and most economic explanation is usually the best one. If Trago had used some drug or some power of hypnotic suggestion, the entire episode of the computer and this cave with the shimmering Wall would become understandable within the more comfortable rules of modern physical science.

Trago said nothing. He merely waited for Deane to answer his own questions.

"Come on, Trago!" Deane challenged. "Do some more of your 'magic.' You know you can't because the spell's broken. Let's see you disappear now!"

Trago studied the linguist with a pained expression. He seemed saddened by Deane's outburst.

"You may believe what you will, scholar," he said finally. "The Wall is more difficult to understand than anything men of knowledge have ever studied. I am sure that your colleagues will agree with your conclusion that this entire episode is nothing but an illusion. Since that is the case, I am sure you will not mind if I leave by the Wall and try to track Aruca."

Deane smiled. "Still at it, huh? O.K., go ahead. Don't let me stop you! Show me how it's done."

Trago walked quickly to the maroon curtain at the end of the bookshelf and passed through it without another glance at Deane, who quickly followed after him. When Trago reached the end of the tunnel, he turned around abruptly.

"Please do not attempt to follow me into the Wall of Mists," he said. "Your doubts would destroy you!"

"You mean they'd destroy your illusion!" Deane scoffed. "I have no intentions of continuing with this charade. I'm not sure why or how you've designed this complex game, but I'll find out!"

The hermit nodded solemnly and wound his way among the carved stelae toward the massive altar in front of the opaque barrier. Just before he stepped into the Wall, he stopped and looked over his shoulder at Deane.

"Whether you believe anything else or not, stay out of the Wall, scholar," he warned. "It is far too dangerous for a novice such as yourself to risk, especially if you do not believe in its power."

Deane studied Trago's stern expression, trying to decide if the old hermit was issuing a veiled threat or if he was merely trying to recapture the illusion of his spent spell. He decided it did not matter.

"I've had enough of this, old man!" he told Trago angrily. "I'm going down this mountain into Monte Azul. That's where you played your first trick on me, in the cantina. I'm going to get to the truth. You must have drugged me, or something, and someone there will tell me!"

Turning, Deane left the Wall of Mists and the old hermit and made his way back through the tunnel into Trago's quarters. Confused theories ran through his mind. Perhaps this was a plan, cooked up by Faranza and Trago both, to pass off the fake Olmec sculptures!

That had to be it! The two of them could discredit Deane, if he tried to expose them! They could claim he was mad! With this thought in mind, he hurriedly picked up the sculpture of the werejaguar and examined it carefully. Once more, its strange beauty struck him. Angry as he was

at Faranza, he had to admit that the man was a skilled artisan. Glancing around the room, Deane walked over to the
crude fireplace and dipped his finger in the black soot.
Then he smeared the soot over the sculpture.

He grinned in triumph, then cursed himself for his own
gullibility.

There was Faranza's "signature" mark—the two tiny
parallel lines with a tiny dot above them.

"That was quite an act you two put on in Monte Azul,"
Deane said to the absent Faranza bitterly. "Now let's see if
we can find out what this elaborate charade is all about."

Thrusting the sculpture in his pocket, Deane made his
way out of the cave, heading for Monte Azul.

Deane burst into the darkened cantina suddenly, his
abrupt entrance startling the bartender. The man squinted
in the dim halflight of the bar, trying to see who it was that
had entered so noisily. Deane saw in relief that it was the
same man who had served the drinks to him and Trago.

"Would the senor like a drink?" the bartender asked as
Deane approached the bar. "The day is hot and—"

"The senor would like to know what was in his drink the
last time he was here!" Deane stated coldly.

The bartender's eyes opened wide in genuine surprise.
"I do not know what you are talking about, Senor. Did it
make you ill? That sometimes happens with *yanquis*. . . ."

Deane was momentarily at a loss. The man was obviously sincere—he was not subtle enough to put on such a
convincing act.

"I'm sorry," Deane said. "I'm not accusing you of tam-
pering with my drink, but perhaps you saw the two men
who were here before I entered put something into it. The
old man, Miguel Trago, and my assistant, Luis Faranza.
You must know Faranza, he spent weeks here!"

The bartender appeared absolutely mystified. "Weeks? Luis Faranza has been in here one or two times, but I never saw the old man before that day you spoke with him. And I never saw them together."

"But that's not possible!" Deane protested. "Faranza's been spending lots of time here, with the women—"

The bartender grinned. "The only woman he ever asked about is some old Zoque woman named Aruca. I told him where she lived, and he seemed very excited." The bartender shrugged. "Excited and . . . frightened, if that is possible."

Deane put his hand to his head. He'd had the mystery all figured out, now it was slipping away from his grasp, just as his own reality—perhaps even his own sanity—was slipping away.

"Wait!" he said suddenly, reaching into his pocket to pull out the piece of fake Olmec art. "Faranza and Trago might have been working on this—"

Deane stopped. His blood grew cold. The statue was gone!

"What is it, Senor?" the bartender asked anxiously. "Are you feeling ill again?"

"N-no," Deane stammered. "I've lost something! I've got to find it!"

Ignoring the bartender's muttered remarks about "crazy *yanquis*," Deane stumbled out of the cantina and began running back up the trail that led to the cave. His eyes searched every foot of the packed clay surface for the figurine of the werejaguar in case it had fallen out of his pocket. But he had not found it by the time he reached the faint path leading into the cavern.

Night had fallen. Pulling out his Bic, Deane flicked on the lighter and made his way into the temple-cave. If things outside the cave appeared different, Deane passed it off, attributing it to the way darkness distorted images sometimes. Groping through the thick undergrowth at the entrance, Deane made his way into the cavern.

Turn to page 181.

THE CHILDREN OF CHAN

It was dark when Deane awoke. The back rear half of his skull felt as if it had split apart. Before he could even focus his eyes, he gingerly probed the massive sore spot where he had been hit behind his ears. Gradually he managed to raise his head and opened one eye.

He was lying in an open enclosure on a sloping hillside. There were at least a dozen figures sitting and lying on the ground around him. Most of them were men, dressed in simple leather breechclouts and vests but also wearing the same hooded capes of jaguar pelts he had seen before his capture. Their hoods were made of the heads and muzzles of the jungle cats, and they wore mittens made of jaguar paws with sharpened claws.

"He is awake, Aruca!" The words were Zoque, and the name sent an electric shiver through Deane's body. Twisting to one side, he raised himself to a sitting position. As the tall, graceful woman walked toward him from the fringe of the enclosure, Deane saw that he was completely surrounded by members of the jaguar cult. The woman stood over him with her arms folded while he tried to focus his unsteady eyes on her face.

"So this is the mighty 'Shutec' of the Huastas!" she challenged. "Look, Children of Chan! Look upon the god whom the prophet Luz has promised will save Talzok from us! See the red blood on his back? And the weakness in his limbs? Should we be frightened of this one man? It is true that he is strong, but most warriors are strong. Luz also warns that he comes to us through the Wall of Red Mists, as if we would be frightened of such a thing!"

The bloodstained cultists laughed at the woman's remarks, pointing at Deane and making crude remarks.

Deane tried to clear his head of the lingering pain from the blows so that he could understand what was being said.

"Kill him, Aruca!"

"No, use the box! Turn him into a snake!"

"Show him the face of Chan!"

Ignoring the warriors, Deane rose on wobbly legs to stand in front of the priestess. "Yes, Aruca," he said quietly. "Show me the face of Chan! Use the blue cube of the Starmen and change your shape, just as you did at Monte Azul. Trago wasn't able to find you, but I did."

Aruca's youthful, tanned face grew pale. "How could you possibly know of these things?" she gasped, taking a step closer to Deane. "Was it the sorcerer, Trago, who broke the vow of silence? Answer me!"

"I will answer you with your own words rather than mine, 'priest-sister of the jaguar-never-die,' " he replied, repeating the obscure Zoque phrase he recorded and translated from her "prayer" at Monte Azul.

The priestess of Chan lurched forward, slapping his bearded mouth with a powerful blow that stunned the weakened scientist. Her followers were on their feet instantly, ready to pierce Deane's body with their deadly obsidian spears, but Aruca raised her hand and shouted a rapid command.

"Bind and gag him, then take him to my hut! He has offended Chan most grievously and must be purified by me alone!"

At least a dozen strong hands grabbed Deane, binding him painfully with leather thongs and wrapping a strip of cloth tightly across his mouth.

Then they lifted him in his arms and carried him off. He caught a glimpse of a thatched roof on top of mud walls only moments before he was tossed roughly on the hard-packed clay floor of Aruca's hut.

"Leave him!" she commanded the cultists. "Remain outside and be prepared to slay him if he runs."

The warriors obeyed their priestess, filing out of the hut's only doorway. Through the thin shade of woven grasses on the single window, Deane could see their tall silhouettes guarding the entrance. Aruca's strong arms encircled his chest and pulled him to a sitting position, propping his back against the hut's center pole. Then she stripped the gag from his mouth.

"None of them should hear my secret will-words, idiot! Those words are more powerful than you know!"

"That's unlikely," Deane replied. "I know all the secrets of the Starmen who taught the people of Chan to use the Wall. How else could I have followed you from Monte Azul to here?"

The bluff was a bold one but—as it turned out—unnecessary. The cult priestess was already cutting the thongs on Deane's wrists and ankles with her ritual dagger.

"You're no Starman, you're just a foolish man of the future who spied on me at Monte Azul," she scoffed. "I had you brought in here because I wanted to silence you when you were repeating my will-words in front of everyone. I already have more than enough reasons to distrust you, though."

"What reasons?" Deane asked.

"When I first learned that you were asking questions about me in Monte Azul, I feared that Trago had found me. Then, when I saw you with the tyrant of Talzok, I was certain that you were another of our enemies. Luz himself called upon you as the god Shutec just before we killed him, so I thought we had captured the evil demon-messiah Luz had been threatening to send among us for so long."

"So Faranza's been dabbling in the black arts as well as tyranny!" Deane thought with a shiver. But he only said,

"Why didn't you just kill Trago, too? Your assassins are powerful and seem to be everywhere, since they also make war against the innocent people of Talzok."

"It is not the people we fight, but their foreign masters, the Huasta!" Aruca said angrily. "Talzok was built by my ancestors, the first Zoque to dwell in the swamp. When the Huasta first came to our land for women and slaves, my people deserted these hills for the safety of the swamp. There they were able to fight the invaders for nearly three generations."

"And then the Huasta conquered you," Deane supplied excitedly. The story was a familiar and timeless one in the histories of primitive states everywhere, but the scientist's mind was racing. He had suddenly realized that he was hearing the true origin of the Olmec culture, the source of all the advanced wisdom and technology of the powerful Maya and Aztec states in later times!

"They conquered our bodies but not our spirits," Aruca replied proudly. "The Huasta killed our men, and even our male babies in a slaughter which made this swamp reek of rotten human flesh for nearly a full year. They took our priests because they had none of their own, castrated them so that their clans would die, and then forced them to serve the Huastecan devils as slave priests. Those were the times before the Wall appeared and the gods were weaker than they are today."

"When did you first learn of the Wall?" Deane asked. "Did the Starmen appear at the same time?"

The priestess sat with her back against the center pole and stared at the wisp of smoke curling upward through the hole in the hut's roof. The firelight softened her hardened facial lines, revealing a subtle wild beauty beneath the vivid jungle colors daubed on her graceful cheeks. Her eyes seemed to melt while the barest hint of smile tilted the

———

204

corners of her unpainted mouth.

"I was but a girl," she began wistfully, lost in a revered memory. "My mother's people had escaped the cruel bloodbath of Talzok and had taken refuge in the hidden caves above the valley. One of my uncles called us to his cave one night to show us something he had just discovered. It was the cavern of the altar, and the Wall of Red Mists was already there."

"But that's impossible!" Deane shook his head. "That had to be at least twenty-five years ago, and you can't be more than twenty now!"

Aruca smiled knowingly. "Perhaps you do not understand the secrets of the Starmen as well as you imagined. You know the words of my prayer but not its effects."

"Effects? Are you saying that the jaguar spell keeps you young?"

"Let me finish the story of the Wall and the Starmen," Aruca said. "Perhaps all of your questions will be answered by then."

"Just one more, please," Deane begged, seeing her eyes flash in irritation. "Do you recall whether anyone had lived in the cave of the Wall before your family hid there?"

He was hoping to find out who had fashioned the secret chamber where he and Faranza had first arrived in the cavern.

Aruca shook her head. "We found some crude stone weapons and tools in the cave," she said. "They were not the well-made instruments of obsidian, like those my people make today. They were made of stone, and looked like the work of children."

Deane nodded. She was describing some of the earliest, crudest stone tools made by the first Indian hunters in Mexico. He doubted that the Wall had been a part of the cave at that time.

Aruca continued, "At first, we were very much afraid of the Wall. It seemed to us to be a living thing, with its heart beat reflected in the throbbing light. We threw stones and spears into it, causing the mists to churn into clouds. My uncle was reaching to touch it when we saw a figure forming among the disturbed clouds. As the mists settled, we could see a tall brown man sitting in a shiny tree of some kind with round things at the bottom."

"Did this creature have a face, with eyes and a nose, and a mouth?" Deane asked.

"Yes, but when it spoke, the mouth did not move like ours," Aruca answered. "It was as if he wore a mask of brown flesh and could talk to us without opening his lips. Some of my people thought that he was a statue carved of wood."

"But did *he* move?" Deane queried.

"Oh, yes, after he changed himself into the god we call Shutec. That was how I knew that the Prophet Luz was lying as soon as I saw you. You are just a man."

"Tell me how the Starman looked," the linguist urged, absorbed in the priestess's story. "Why do you think he changed?"

"He saw that we were trembling and began to change so that we would not fear his presence," she answered.

"And you saw him change?" Deane demanded. "Just as I saw you change into a jaguar?"

The priestess nodded. "He remained inside the Wall until he had become like our men. Then he stepped from the mists, naked and strong, like a god. His hair and beard were golden red, like yours, but he was much taller, as tall as the Prophet Luz. He held a small box of blue glass in his hand and looked into it whenever he talked to us. That is how he taught us to use the will-words for changing."

"Did the box make any sounds when he talked to you?"

Aruca was quiet for several long moments. Finally she cocked her head to one side. "I don't remember," she said softly, almost in a puzzled tone of voice. "The Blue Cube would start to glow with the red light, just like the Wall. Then the Starman's words suddenly appeared in my thoughts. I guess I thought he spoke them, because how else could they have gotten there? Anyway, I just knew about the changing and the Wall, and all of my kinspeople did too."

"A telepathic communicator!" Deane thought "Perhaps a portable version of the Wall!"

"Did the lessons explain how the changing worked?" he asked Aruca, trying to hide his mounting excitement. What a scientific discovery *this* was!

"I only remember that the will-words were placed in my thoughts then and that I have never forgotten them. We all understood that we could stop time from flowing by using our special will-words to take a different form, and we could travel backward and forward in time through the Wall. The Starman left then and took the Blue Cube with him."

Deane did not understand everything she was saying, but was beginning to realize that there was little or no actual relationship between the Wall of Mists and the were-jaguar cult. For some unknown reason, the mysterious Starmen had taught the Zoque refugees how to slow the aging process considerably by taking the shape of other life-forms. They could then use the Wall to travel through the millenia to different stages of their lives. The use of these changeling powers by the Children of Chan to fight the Huasta and their renegade priests was probably not connected to the "Starmen" at all. The Children of Chan had simply taken advantage of their unique powers to battle a much stronger enemy.

"Who is Trago?" Deane asked, suddenly wondering about the relationship between the hermit and the priestess. "Is he your brother, as he claims to be?"

"Brother?" Aruca exclaimed angrily. "How could such an evil man be my brother? No, Trago is not my kinsman. He is my enemy! He is a sorcerer and a human leech who lives by the deaths of others!"

"What do you mean?" Deane asked, startled.

"Trago was a sorcerer in our tribe. He learned the secret of the Wall from one of my kinswomen who broke our vow of silence in a foolish moment of passion. He used my sister's wish-word to change into another form so that he could remain young."

"What's so evil about that?" asked Deane. "That's what you and the other Children of Chan do."

"My followers and I are not sorcerers!" Aruca hissed furiously. "We only take *animal* forms! The spell exhausts the life force of these animals, so we forbid the taking of human forms."

Shuddering, Deane began to understand. He stared at Aruca in horror. "But Trago did, didn't he! He took a human body!"

"Yes! He first stole the body of my sister, who loved him. Then he used her body to entice young men of each generation to his lair. There he stole and used their bodies. When I discovered what he was doing, I tried to kill him, but he escaped through the Wall. Since then, I have followed him, vowing to put an end to his evil."

"So *you* have been hunting Trago!" Deane exclaimed. "He told me just the reverse—that he was tracking you through the Wall of Mists!"

The priestess nodded. "That is why I was so afraid of you at first. Trago tries sometimes to return here in the stolen body of a younger human from the future, and he often chooses one which will frighten us. I thought it was possible that you were Trago, himself, following me from Monte Azul, where he has been hiding for the past two years."

Deane remembered the hermit's bony hands on his arm in the ritual cavern and he broke out in a cold sweat. With an effort, he forced his mind to consider Aruca's explanation.

"Then Trago has terrorized both Huastec and Zoque in this time, and has become too notorious to remain here in his own form?"

Aruca smiled sadly. "Trago is a very wise sorcerer. He knows how to disguise himself and avoid capture, but he must also remain close to the Wall in order to escape whenever we find him. Even now, my changeling warriors are seeking him through the Mists. If they kill him, all traces of his evil works will vanish from that point onward in time. It would be best, of course, if we could attract him back to our own time and kill him here."

"Is that why you didn't kill him in Monte Azul?" Deane persisted. "Were you trying to lure him back to an earlier time to assassinate him with the greatest effects?"

Aruca's beautiful face wrinkled in a puzzled scowl. "No," she replied. "He had somehow learned that I was near and escaped just before I arrived. I tracked him to your house at Kaktunque, where I spied on you for several days. When it seemed clear that you were not Trago in a new body, I thought I had lost his trail once more, and returned here."

A sudden thought made Deane gasp. The final pieces of the puzzle were falling into place all around him.

"What is the matter?" Aruca demanded fearfully.

"Nothing!" Deane whispered. "Nothing at all! I think Trago's evil has ended forever!"

"You are mad?" Aruca said scornfully.

"No, not anymore!" Deane breathed gratefully. Bending over, he etched two parallel lines in the clay floor of the hut, topping it with a circle "Does this mark mean anything to you?" he asked Aruca

He heard a sharp intake of air from Aruca. "That is Trago's secret mark," she said in a quivering voice "He uses it to identify his followers How did you know about this unless . . ."

"Relax, Aruca. I'm not one of Trago's followers, even if I have been living with him for the past two years! You see, I knew him as a man named 'Faranza'' '

Deane paused, enjoying the waves of understanding which swept into his mind. Trago and Faranza were the same person! It explained everything! The tampered computer program, the secret chamber behind the Wall of Mists, even the flawless Olmec style of Faranza's sculptures. They were genuine Olmec artifacts!

"I should have guessed it sooner," Deane murmured more to himself than to Aruca. "Everything pointed to him. He and Trago were never in the same place at the same time! I even saw him, red-faced, changing his clothes after I had been talking to him as 'Miguel Trago!' Logically, he was the only person who could have tampered with either my computer or its program, and he was the only other Zoque speaker I knew! He tried to hide his language abilities when he appeared as Faranza, but then he 'learned' your language faster than he should have. Even in the cave behind the Wall, he was the one who told me we were locked in from the *inside,* and I believed him!"

The priestess shook her head. "I don't know what you're talking about. Your words are future words and they confuse me. I still do not see what this has to do with our quest for Trago."

"He used me, Aruca! He took the old hermit's form in Monte Azul just long enough to suck me into his plan to escape from you. Now I know why he started staying away from Kaktunque. He knew you were close to him and needed to finish whatever he was working on in the cave before you arrived."

The priestess's dark eyes were still frowning as if she were having trouble understanding the cause of Deane's elation.

"Don't you see!" Deane cried. "He's dead! Trago used my computer to return here in the only disguise you might not penetrate—a giant, insane prophet from the future, one who terrorized your people by dressing in their skins! It was Luz, Aruca! He was Faranza, and Faranza was Trago. The Children of Chan have many reasons to rejoice tonight!"

Aruca stared at Deane for a moment thoughtfully, then slowly nodded her head. "Yes, that makes sense." Her eyes closed in thankfulness. "The evil sorcerer is finally dead." Then, lifting her gaze, she looked at Deane and smiled shyly. "You do look a bit like the Starman when he became a god, except that you are smaller and I can hear your voice. I could not touch the giant from the stars, but I can touch you."

Deane saw that Aruca's face was blushing beneath the painted designs. She moved closer to him.

"Aren't you too old for me?" he teased. "Aren't you about three thousand and two years old?"

Aruca smiled. "The spell of the Starmen works only to delay one's death. It does not make us immortal, although that is what we thought at first. The Wall allows us to travel to the different ages of our lives, but does not prevent us from growing old."

"Then are you twenty or three thousand years old right

now?" Deane asked, confused.

"Both," she replied easily. "Time does not pass away like the wood in a fire. It is always there, just as the space we fill. By using the wish-word, I can will myself to take my own body as it appears at any particular time. I could not look this young at the time I spied on Trago at Monte Azul, because my body was over three thousand years old! Here, it is only sixty-two and appears the same as it did when I first saw the Wall, thanks to the power of the Starmen's will-words."

Deane heard her words, but did not grasp what she meant until much later. All he knew now was that he could return to his own time whenever he chose, by way of the Wall of Mists, or he might learn how to convert his computer into a portable version of the Wall by using digitalized spellwords, as Faranza-Trago had done.

"What are you thinking?" asked Aruca. The priestess's primal beauty excited him, diverting his thoughts quickly from computers and Walls. She might accompany him into the future, to his own time, but she would forfeit her youth and be required to survive as a werejaguar if she did.

"I was thinking of the future, Aruca, and of how the present links it with the past," he said, reaching for the flap on the window of the hut. He would postpone his ultimate choice for another night.

Removing her jaguar cowl, the priestess threw it into a darkened corner of the hut and drew near the golden-haired stranger whom the Huasta had thought was a god.

THE END

EPILOGUE

The startling discoveries in Trago's cave confused Steven Deane even more than his earlier experience with the computer. He spent three weeks in Kaktunque, trying unsuccessfully to finish the literacy report for the Mexican government in an absent-minded way. Luckily, most of the work had already been done. His three-day absence had gone unnoticed by the villagers, who were accustomed to the American's strange behavior and irregular hours.

As he expected, no one asked about the large Mayan. Luis Faranza had always been a lone operator in his sculpture forgery business and had no friends.

Deane discovered his notebooks and other materials were still in his hut, along with his collection of research diskettes. He had accumulated more than enough field data to finish his work on the Zoque highlanders but was already feeling the disappointment of having discovered something no one would believe without adequate proof. Even *he* was beginning to wonder . . .

Finally Deane gave up trying to work. The weird events of the past month went round and round in his mind until he was afraid he would go mad. "Perhaps I'm already mad!" he thought grimly. Fortunately, he was still sane enough to know that it would be useless to remain in Mexico. His literacy data was good enough to finish the government report in Boston, and would provide sufficient material for several staid academic articles on Mayan linguistic history.

He was not sorry to leave Monte Azul and return to the "real" world of Mexico City. The plane that would take him back to the United States would not leave until 6:30 that evening. Deane had nearly twelve hours to kill, and he knew that trying to sleep was useless. He had not been able to sleep soundly for weeks, ever since—

Deane forced his thoughts away from that treadmill. To keep himself occupied, he decided to visit the Zoque exhibit at the Museum Nacional, to photograph some of the artifacts for illustrations in his final report.

When the museum opened at eight o'clock in the morning, Deane was the first visitor. He presented his credentials to the curator's secretary, who seemed reluctant at first to admit this nervous American with wild, bloodshot eyes.

But, finally, he was allowed open access to the Zoque materials, and started selecting the best items for his purposes. It was a design on a large burial urn that finally provided him the ultimate key to the intertwined mysteries of the Olmec sculptures and his Monte Azul experiences.

He was moving the pot into position for photographing, when he suddenly noticed a series of parallel dashes and dots around the rim of a red and brown burial pot. These were almost like the calendar marks of Olmec and Classic Maya stelae. The same kind of marks also appeared on various embroidered cloths, wooden implements, and other pieces of Zoque pottery. Deane began to study the design, fascinated by the way such a simple feature could have spread so rapidly to neighboring Indian groups. He had just begun taking the first photographs when he realized this calendar design was just a slightly modified version of Luis Faranza's signature mark!

Suddenly excited, he replaced the Zoque materials in their protective cases and hurried to find the museum's large Olmec collection. He remembered Faranza's boast that his counterfeit pieces might one day be placed in the best museum collections—perhaps it had already happened! In the Olmec room, he began to browse among the smaller items, looking for the telltale marks. It was in the second case that he saw it.

Among a collection of ceremonial jade axeheads, there was one with a bearded head etched on its side. The Olmecs were known for their bearded figures, which had led some experts to believe that their high culture had been introduced by a non-Indian group with more facial hair. In this case, the bearded person wore a feathered headdress, the common symbol for either a priest or a god. And just above the feathers was a clearly etched equal sign with a dot above it!

The card in the exhibit case did not provide any information on the source of the items, but Deane knew that the curator's office would have such records in their files. He noted the tiny acquisition number penned on the axe and copied it into his notebook before moving on to the other displays.

For the next four hours, Deane examined every Olmec artifact in the museum and found seventeen pieces signed by Faranza's secret mark! For each one, he recorded the acquisition number and a brief description of the item. Finally, he returned to the curator's office and requested access to the museum's list of donors. The suspicious secretary was even cooler than before to the disheveled scientist, offering him an unused desk near her own so that she keep an eye on him.

Deane flipped through the computer printout of the acquisitions list that provided a detailed description of each piece, including any available information about its origin. At first he could not believe what he was reading and had to check and doublecheck each reference number.

Only four of the seventeen artifacts with Faranza's coded signature had been added to the Museum's collection within the past ten years! Practically every other piece of Olmec art had been excavated by well-documented archeological expeditions during the twenties and thirties, several decades before Luis Faranza had even been born!

"Pardon me, Senora, but there must be something wrong with these numbers," Deane called to the secretary.

She glanced at him with a frown. "I'm quite sure that the numbers are accurate, Senor Deane," she said primly. "Our staff is most meticulous regarding such matters. If you have any further questions, perhaps you should discuss them with the Cataloging Office."

"I'd like that very much," said Deane, "if you would be kind enough to arrange an appointment."

The matronly woman pursed her lips and turned away from Deane to use the intercom. She spoke quickly in Spanish to someone named Gustez on the other end, then nodded brusquely to the American.

"Dr. Gustez will see you now," she informed him. "Room 312."

"May I take this acquisitions list with me for reference?" he asked, patting the thick printout.

The secretary brushed an imaginary strand of iron grey hair from her thickly powdered forehead. "Cataloging will have their own copy of that document, Senor Deane. We do not allow such materials to leave their assigned offices."

The corners of her mouth had tilted slightly in a wry smile. She seemed to welcome her first opportunity to deny something to the wild-eyed American. Deane didn't notice, he was already on his way to the door.

The third floor of the Museum Nacional was taken entirely by research offices that resembled the offices of individual professors in American university departments. The Cataloging Office occupied an entire wing on the west side of the third floor. The main door opened onto a busy room with a dozen clerical workers using telephones and pressing keys on computer terminals. The receptionist was a pleasant young woman who spoke very little English.

She paid no attention to the linguist's appearance, perhaps more accustomed than the Curator's secretary to dealing with field workers. "Professor Gustez expects you," she said brightly after he introduced himself in Spanish. "It is the door by the stairs at the end of the hall."

Deane thanked her and followed her directions to an unmarked door he had just passed.

"Come in!" a man's muffled voice yelled in response to his knock.

Opening the door, Deane found himself in a large room filled with row after row of metal utility shelves like the ones in library stacks. Most of them were crowded with large cardboard boxes with code numbers on the outside end.

"Back here!" called the voice, still sounding somewhat muffled. Deane followed the sound until he reached a series of heavy tables placed against a row of outer windows. The tables were cluttered with bits and pieces of archeological discoveries, ranging from tiny potsherds to a massive stone column with Aztec characters. He also saw lettering kits, labels, microscopes, and several computer terminals, the cataloging tools of modern museums. The chairs and stools in front of the tables were all empty.

"Here I am," said a voice behind him, no longer muffled. A dapper little man in a white laboratory coat was shutting a door with "FOTOGRAFIA" stenciled on it. He was carrying a plastic specimen bag with what seemed to be fragments of straw.

"I'm Roberto Gustez," he greeted the linguist with an outstretched hand. He spoke in American English with practically no accent. "I understand that you've been studying Zoque near Monte Azul, Dr. Deane. What can I do for you?"

Deane did not respond immediately, wondering how he might suggest that some of the Museum's most valuable pieces were frauds without creating an official furor that could delay his departure this evening. Finally he decided to be straightforward.

"I came here to get some photographs of some Zoque artifacts to illustrate a report, but that's not why I asked to see you, Dr. Gustez. While I was studying the collection downstairs, I noticed something very disturbing that I want to show you."

Sensing the tension and seriousness in Deane's manner, Gustez motioned for him to sit at the table. The professor's well-scrubbed face and hands might have belonged to a hospital physician as he leaned closer to the exhausted linguist.

"What's the matter, Dr. Deane? Have you been taking drugs?"

"No! Nothing like that!" Deane protested, flushing. "I've just finished a long period of field work and I'm very tired. I—I've had a lot of trouble sleeping since my return."

"Then what is it you wish to show me?"

"Let me begin simply by saying that a man I hired in Merida made his living by counterfeiting Olmec artifacts. He used a special signature symbol, almost as a private joke, to distinguish his work from authentic pieces."

"Olmec?" Gustez replied, his crisp black moustache bristling. "That is the biggest market these days for fraudulent antiquities. We estimate that as many as fifty percent of the artifacts sold as 'Olmec' to tourists are counterfeit. What does this have to do with us?"

Deane handed the professor his notebook, turning it to the page with the catalog numbers. "Every one of these artifacts have the secret signature mark on them that I told you about, Dr. Gustez. I have just checked the master catalog in the curator's office and learned that most of them were acquired by the Museum during the early twentieth century. That means someone has been stealing your original artifacts and replacing them with Faranza's copies."

Gustez frowned and scanned the list, along with Deane's hasty descriptions of each item. "I know these artifacts, Dr. Deane. Some of them are among my favorites in the Olmec collection, and I have studied them very closely. What is this 'signature mark' you have seen?"

"Here," said Deane, pulling a pen from his shirt. "I'll show you." He leaned closer to the table and quickly sketched a neat equal sign with a dot centered over it. Then he pointed to the page. "That's it. It's almost microscopic on some of the articles but it's there. And it's identical to the marks I watched this man making!"

Gustez smiled immediately as soon as he saw the design Deane had drawn. "Ah! The calendar mark! You are right in one way, Dr. Deane. Those marks are indeed on many of the Olmec pieces in the Museum, but they have always been there. Here, it's my turn to show you something."

The professor went to a large bookshelf near the photographic laboratory and found a bulky looseleaf portfolio. Returning to the table, he laid the big folder on top of everything already there. Then he untied the laces which held the portfolio together and began thumbing through the stiff pages of old museum photographs. He seemed to know exactly what he was looking for and stopped when he found it.

"There!" he said emphatically, pointing to a series of photographs of the axe with the bearded man Deane had noticed in the exhibit. "Observe that the catalog number is the same as the one in your notebook, and also look at the date on the photograph."

Deane studied the page carefully, verifying that this artifact and the one he had studied were the same. There was an excellent closeup of the design on the axeblade, surprisingly well-lighted for a photograph that old. Faranza's signature mark was perfectly visible just above the feathered headdress, and the date on the photograph was 'September 18th, 1927'!" The scientist felt his face go stiff with shock.

"I can show you more photographs from that same period, just after we began to seek Olmec materials openly, Dr. Deane. You will find that mark on most of them. In fact, I have written a paper for the Society for Mexican Archaeology on that subject. You may have a copy of it if you wish. In it, I call that design a 'calendar mark' and suggest that it be regarded as an important method of identifying true Olmec antiquities because it appears on so many of them."

Deane looked away from the professor, staring out the window high above the morning traffic in Mexico's capital. Once again he saw Faranza's thick fingers manipulate the small dental pick as he carved a similar axe from Monte Azul jade.

"I would like to meet this man you call 'Faranza,' Dr. Deane. Oh, not to have him arrested," Gustez added quickly. "Good quality reproductions of Olmec artifacts are treasures in their own right. It is only the collector who is damaged by such people. Your former assistant sounds like a skilled artisan. I am impressed that he noticed the same mark that I did and recognized its importance. It might be difficult even for me to distinguish a well-made Olmec counterfeit from a genuine artifact if it carried the calendar mark!"

Deane shook his head, too stunned to speak more than a

mumbled apology for taking the professor's time. He started to leave but Gustez stopped him.

"Wait! Let me show you one more thing which will interest you." The fastidious researcher disappeared for a minute or two and returned carrying one of the large boxes from the metal shelves.

"This material is the first shipment from one of the first Olmec excavations near Monte Azul," he explained. "The artifacts in this box have not been cleaned or cataloged except for temporary processing in the field over fifty years ago. The entire collection was discovered in our basement only last week. It was considered lost for more than half a century! I have already seen the items and have noticed one very special figure."

Deane felt the sinking feeling only moments before Gustez handed him the jade werejaguar that the scientist had last seen in Trago's cave. He did not need to see Faranza's mark to know the Mayan had made it, because it was still vividly outlined by the soot he himself had rubbed into it from the hermit's cave. But it had vanished from his hand. Or had it? Deane didn't know—he didn't care. It was the one shred of evidence Deane needed to preserve his own sanity—and to prove that Luis Faranza and Miguel Trago were the same individuals!

". . . from a grave beyond the site," the professor was saying. "It seems to have been in a fire at some time, or at least rubbed with ashes. Possibly part of a ritual. You can see that the calendar mark is obvious, and this was dug from a tomb much older than your counterfeiter. We are just beginning to survey the mountains above Monte Azul, looking for undiscovered cave sites which may contain our most important clues to the origin of the Olmec culture."

The American smiled and nodded absently. He was trying to visualize the scene inside Trago's temple cave when this dapper scientist, or one like him, stumbled into the secret chamber and found the portable computer. Faranza had been right all along. His sculptures were being circulated throughout the world as Olmec originals—which they were, after all!

THE END

ABOUT THE AUTHOR

Morris Simon is a middle-aged kid, who does odd jobs such as college teaching and private consulting to support his writing and computing habits. In one world, he's a practicing anthropologist with a Ph.D. from Cornell; in another one, he writes science fiction and fantasy, microcomputer books and articles, and interactive novels.

JAGUAR! is his tenth interactive book in the last three years. Most of the others have been published by TSR, Inc., in their ENDLESS QUEST® paperback book series. Simon likes to incorporate factual archeological and anthropological material in his books—such as the widespread werejaguar cult of Central America. Simon is currently working on several dozen varied fiction and nonfiction projects while he and his wife, Sherry, grow children in Alabama.

AMAZING™ STORIES:

60 Years of the Best Science Fiction

Edited by Isaac Asimov and Martin H. Greenberg

This anthology features some of the best stories from the early days of America's first and longest-running science-fiction magazine, **AMAZING®
Science Fiction Stories**. This trade paperback book is enhanced by full-color reproductions of sixteen covers photographed from the original magazines.

The anthology includes stories published as early as 1928. Some of the authors represented are Isaac Asimov, Ursula K. Le Guin, John Jakes, Philip José Farmer, Robert Bloch, and Philip K. Dick.

240 pages • $7.95   **JUNE 1985**

Distributed to the book trade in the U.S. by Random House, Inc., and in Canada by Random House of Canada, Ltd.